GUNSHOTS IN THE NIGHT!

Spur woke with a start just after 1 A.M. when twin blasts from a shotgun roared into his room, ripping apart the bedding. He shook his head to clear out the ringing and crawled to the window. He saw a man dropping off the end of a rope and jumping onto a horse.

Spur was damned glad he had made a dummy out of his carpetbag and a spare blanket. He was glad it had been the dummy in his bed instead of him.

The gunman's mistake played right into Spur's hands. Things had been getting hot for him in Durango, and now things would cool down—

Because as far as anyone knew, Spur McCoy was dead!

(Cover   )

Also in the SPUR series by Dirk Fletcher

SPUR #4

ROCKY MOUNTAIN VAMP

Dirk Fletcher

LEISURE BOOKS ⚮ NEW YORK CITY

A LEISURE BOOK

Published by

Dorchester Publishing Co., Inc.
41 E. 60 St.
New York City

Printed in the United States of America

CHAPTER ONE

Ed Bainbridge had just left the door of his rough log cabin when a sledgehammer blow jolted his right shoulder, spun him backward and dumped him in a heap beside the woodpile. The sound came almost at once, a sharp, stinging report of a rifle close by, and he knew he had been bushwhacked. Ed fought down a sudden blackness as the pain from his shoulder cascaded into his brain. His right hand grabbed at the wound and he gurgled in agony when he touched his arm. It was hit bad. He shook his head to clear away the heavy dark mists that settled over him. Slowly he drove them back, blinked and pulled out his Colt Peacemaker. He had fallen into a spot behind the wood where he figured the attackers couldn't see him.

He was lucky that way or he'd be dead by now. A rifle that close probably meant rawhiders, men who robbed, looted and killed anyone they came across for money, food and anything they could sell. But he wasn't dead and he didn't intend to be.

Ed was lanky and tall, Texas bred and Texas tough. But Valerie wasn't. His wife was in the cabin and she must have heard the rifle shot. She would know it was a long gun. He prayed she would stay put. He couldn't risk calling to her. If he played possum the rawhiders might think he was dead, and then when they got close enough . . .

Another rifle slug chipped wood an inch over his head. Then a third one bored in from what he guessed was a different angle. He waited.

In the brush surrounding the small mountain clearing, Mort Sawtell lay in the high grass watching the woodpile.

"Dammit, Chug," he said softly. "You just winged the bastard. Now you got to go in there and dig him out."

Chug Rollins scowled, sighted in on the pile of split pine where he had seen the homesteader vanish and threw in a shot. It brought no results. Chug shrugged. He was a slender, short man not over twenty, with a scraggly beard, one tooth missing in front and a nose that constantly ran. He snuffled, wiped a dirty wool shirt sleeve across his wet nose and spat out a stream of brown juice.

"Hail, no problem, Mort. You just watch a real artist doing his job." Chug crawled back to the tree line, then stood and ran for the horses.

Chug mounted his roan and walked her to the edge of the trees. Damn little place. Small cabin, a shack out back, one shed and two lean-tos. He could get between the house and the woodpile and throw three shots into

6

the guy before he knew what happened.

Chug walked the horse into the open, sure the jasper wouldn't try a long shot even for the horse. As Chug got closer he swung on the left side of the horse to provide a smaller target and kicked the mount into a gallop. At the last moment he swung into the saddle, leaned over and fired once past the split wood where he saw the man crouched. The bullet hit home and smashed through the homesteader's right shoulder, spilling the pistol from his hand.

Chug screamed at once. "Got the bastard! Come on in!" Chug dismounted and kicked the wounded man in the side when he tried to stand, toppling him onto the woodpile. Chug grabbed the Peacemaker. Mort walked into the clearing with his gun ready.

From the other side of the buildings the third man came warily. He had a Sharps repeating rifle ready. At forty-two he was the oldest of the three; he wore fringed buckskins and a three-cornered hat. Everybody said that Tom Elliott was crazy. He had one eye that never would look a man head on. His other eye was an empty socket laced with scar tissue. An Indian arrow had done it, Tom said. Actually he had lost it in a barroom brawl in Abilene ten years ago. A thumb had popped it right out of his head and left it dangling on his cheek. Tom had promptly killed the man who did it with one shot.

Chug kicked the homesteader in his wounded shoulder and grinned when the man screeched with pain.

"Well, now the skinny bastard is alive. You hadn't moved just as I shot, you wouldn't had to suffer this way. Just lay there where you are. Nice weapon, that Colt Peacemaker. Damn, I can use that."

Ed tried to sit up, but both of his arms burned with an

7

unrelenting fiery pain.

"What do you want?" he asked.

Tom Elliott laughed, a high cackle, and the other two joined in. He wiped his eyes with a greasy shirt sleeve. "Hail, man, you know fucking well what we want. First we want that little woman you got inside, and then we want that gold dust you been panning, and last we want your horses and your supplies of grub. Don't look like you in too good a shape to stop us."

"Don't hurt Valerie."

"So the cunt's name is Valerie," Chug said. "I damn well get to be first this time, you promised me last time."

Ed felt a dank chill down his spine. They were raw-hiders and life meant nothing to them, less than nothing.

"Look, I've got two bags of gold dust. I been panning at it for almost a year. It's yours. Take it and you can live high in Durango for a year."

"Or what, gold panner?" Elliott said.

"Just take the dust and leave us alone. We won't come after you." Ed saw them thinking about it. They might not be able to find the dust if they killed him. He knew Valerie was listening. He just hoped she didn't do anything outlandish. The woman had a temper.

"Son, you won't be coming after us. Old Tom Elliott can guarantee you that. Not if you can't walk." The .45 slug smashed into Ed's kneecap, shattered his knee bones into a jumbled mass of white splinters and blood, capped by a murderous scream from Ed Bainbridge just before he passed out.

Another shot exploded into the still mountain air. A big .50-caliber lead slug broke the small cabin window, flew straight ahead and caught Tom Elliott in the chest, drove a half inch of rib bone ahead of it as it rammed into his heart and exploded out his back, splattering the woodpile with fragments of bone, blood and human tissue. Tom Elliott threw his hands in the air as he fell, surprise on his already dead face.

Chug whirled, drew the Peacemaker from his belt and fired five shots through the window. Mort had darted toward the cabin and flattened himself next to the door. As soon as the pistol shots ended behind him, Mort kicked the door open and charged inside the one-room log house, his six-gun ready.

Valerie was still kneeling below the window, her arms over her head to ward off the spraying glass. An old Sharps rifle lay at her feet. Mort grabbed her by the wrist and pulled her outside.

"Come on, bitch, you done killed Tom. You come and look at what you did, then that man of yours is gonna see what we do to you."

Chug bent over Tom as they came out of the cabin.

"Old Tom done shot his last man," Chug said. "Clean through the heart. That's some sharpshooter you got there, Mort."

"Don't hurt her!" Ed screamed. "I'll give you the gold. Take it and leave."

Chug swung his six-gun, crashing it into Ed Bainbridge's face, breaking his jaw, driving him sideways over the stack of split wood into the dirt.

"Don't!" Valerie screamed, trying to run to him.

"You worry 'bout yourself, bitch," Mort growled. His hand caught the top of her brown and white gingham dress and jerked downward. Seams parted, cloth tore and the dress and petticoats ripped, came free and hung at her waist. Only a thin, soft chemise covered her breasts. Valerie tried to hold it but Mort grabbed it and ripped it off her. She shrank back. He grabbed her arms and pulled them apart. Her breasts were small, with narrow pink areolas around small pink nipples.

"Please don't!" she said.

"Yeah, we'll get to you. Just two of us but we take turns at everything. Come over here." They stopped in front of where her husband lay in the dirt. He bled from all three wounds and could barely lift his head. Chug held Valerie while Mort slapped her twice, slamming her head from one side to the other.

"You fucking, murdering bitch! You just killed our friend. You hear me?" He grabbed both her breasts and twisted them until she screamed in pain.

"No, you sons-of-bitches!" Ed Bainbridge said, struggling up on one foot, swinging a stick of firewood at them with his painful right arm.

Mort spun around and kicked out hard, his boot landing in Ed's crotch, smashing his testicles, dumping him onto the ground. Mort grabbed Ed and lifted his head.

"Bastard, you got one minute to tell us where that gold is. You don't and we gonna cut one tit off your woman. You hear me?"

Slowly Ed shook his head to clear it. "I hear," he said through his broken jaw. "Don't cut her."

Chug had out his six-inch blade, slender as a filleting knife; it was the one he shaved with. He laid the cold steel on her breast and grinned.

"Where's the fucking gold?" Mort asked.

Ed Bainbridge knew it didn't matter. He was a dead man, and Valerie was dead or worse. Maybe he could make it easier for her. "Gold . . . under stone step, in old jar."

Mort ran to the wide stone in front of the door, took the axe and dug a hole, then pried up the rock. There in a hollow spot lay a jar, more than half filled with gold dust.

"Christ, Chug, look at this. A pint of gold dust. Christ, we're both rich!"

He brought it to Chug, who still held the woman.

"Look at that! You know what that will buy us in Denver?"

"Anything we want!" Chug paused. "What about him? We done with him, ain't we? It's your turn, dammit."

Mort Sawtell nodded, drew his .44 and put two bullets into Ed's chest. Bainbridge died with a scream of protest roaring out of his throat. Valerie had thought it would all work out somehow, but now she watched Ed die and she screamed at the men, wanting to kill the other two, but her body wouldn't obey her. The man behind her held her too tightly, one hand over her breast. She screamed again, a wailing cry of anguish, hatred and terror—and then she fainted.

When Valerie came back to consciousness, she gasped and shot open her eyes. She was in the cabin, spread-eagled and tied to the bed. She was naked. For a moment she wanted to turn her head to hide her shame. She could have at least fought for the right to keep her clothing. Now she was totally at their mercy.

She knew Ed was dead, she knew it but her mind wouldn't accept it. There was only so much tragedy the human spirit could stand. She felt hands on her and looked up. The younger of the two killers stood beside the bed, naked. Her eyes went to his crotch, then looked away. Turning her eyes away wouldn't help her any. She knew it.

"No way you can fight much now, pretty kitten," Chug said. "Not much chance you can keep me out of you, is there?'' He grinned and she memorized every detail of his ugly face. She would remember it forever, or until she killed him, until she saw him die slowly and with as much pain as possible. Then he knelt between her thighs, and she thought automatically of Ed. He was the only man who had ever been there, had ever made love to her, and she screamed. Valerie screamed until his hand shut off the sound and she felt him fall on top of her, probing. Just before he entered her, Valerie Bainbridge fainted again.

The next four hours were a living nightmare for Valerie. She had long spells of consciousness, then would faint again. She knew that both men had their way with her two or three times each. She was sore and messy, felt dirty and ugly, and when she could she shouted at them, screamed until her voice gave out.

It was about noon when they both were dressed again. They had looted the cabin, taking new clothes and almost all the dry food that she had, choosing new cooking pots to load on one of the Bainbridge horses that they would use as a pack animal. Outside she heard shots and one of the horses screaming, evidently in a death struggle.

Chug came in and cut her bonds. He stared at her.

''We never had no woman with us. Would help us some. You got a choice now, woman. You can come with us, cook for us, do our mending and such. Course you got to lay down and spread your legs whenever we say. Or you can stay here with your dead husband.''

''I wouldn't go across the clearning with you rawhiders, you murdering cutthroats!'' She flew at him, one hand reaching his face, where her fingernails scraped flesh raw down one cheek.

''Bitch!'' He slapped her, knocking her down on the

12

bed. He shook his head. "Too damn bad, you was a good fuck. What the hell—with women and horses, you always find one when you need one."

He lifted his .44 and shot Valerie Bainbridge as she lay on the bed. Then he smelled smoke.

"Come on, Chug, I got it burning. Let's go!" Mort yelled.

Chug stared at the girl. His shot had been a little high. It went in just under her shoulder over one breast. It should kill her. Cut into her lung, yeah, she'd die slow. If the bullet didn't do it the damn fire would. He turned and ran out the door, jumped on his horse as Mort held it, and they rode away with two pack horses trailing as they headed for the closest town—Durango!

Inside the burning cabin, Valerie came back to the conscious world, felt the pain in her chest and knew she should get up. The cabin was on fire, burning. She was afraid of fire. She tried to sit up, closed her eyes and cried. She didn't think she would ever make it. Then she fainted again, sprawled naked on the big bed.

CHAPTER TWO

The railroad simply did not go there.

Even with the sprouting of steel rails in dozens of places throughout the West, there were no shining ribbons of steel that went to Durango in the far southwestern section of Colorado. Spur McCoy had at last worked his way to Grand Junction, halfway up the territory of Colorado and some twenty-five miles from the Utah border. The stage line didn't go south from there. He bought a solid, deep-chested black mare and a light saddle. Spur had been over this territory before. He'd take the Gunnison River trail south, moving upstream until the waterway turned east. From then on he'd use dead reckoning and strike out for Mount Wilson, a 14,250-foot peak that loomed in the sky just north of Durango. That made it a hundred-and-fifty-mile ride. Because of the altitude and the rugged going, he allowed four days for the trip. He was at 4,583-feet elevation at Grand Junction and would be climbing most of the way to Mount Wilson, then would drop down to Durango at 6,505 feet, well over a mile in the sky.

Spur McCoy sat now on a ridge not five miles from the Colorado city he was aiming at. It had been a tougher trip than he had guessed. He was in his fifth day, and it was almost noon. He had seen it a half mile back, just the wisp of a trail of light-colored smoke, then as he crested the ridge he saw that it was much more than a lightning-set snag smoldering. It was a real fire, perhaps a cabin. He had seen few signs of habitation in the rugged Rocky Mountains over the past three days. This smoke came from less than half a mile away, just over another low ridge and near a stream he had been counting on to lead him down to the Animas River and on to Durango. Spur kicked the black in the flanks and quartered the slope of the ridge faster than his usual pace, closing the distance to the smoke quickly.

Spur came out of the fringe of trees to the small clearing on the edge of the stream and saw that the cabin had been made of logs and now was almost burned to the ground. The smaller outbuildings were intact and he saw a dead horse near a pole corral. Lying near a woodpile was a man who wasn't moving. Spur left his saddle in one quick leap and glued himself behind a large pine tree. He checked the scene again, looking for movement, for signs of life, for anyone who might still be defending the place. He sprinted to a tree closer to the cabin and looked again. Nothing. No sign of life. But he still wasn't walking in uninvited until he made sure.

"Hello!" he called. "Hello, the cabin. Is anyone there? Can I help you?" He waited a minute and then called again with the same offer. At last he drew his .44

and worked around the tree and ran to the closest shed. Then he ran to the next shed. Nobody was in either. He held the .44 as he ran around the cabin and its smoldering logs, then at last checked the man at the woodpile.

As he did he saw a woman's bare back. She lay half on the man's legs and had been hidden by the wood. He moved and saw the rest of her. She was naked. He ran up and touched the man's throat. His body was cooling, dead an hour, perhaps two. Spur's hand touched the woman's shoulder and she groaned.

She was alive. Spur turned her over gently, moving the wood, and saw at once the bluish bullet hole just below her right collarbone. He'd seen that kind of shot kill more than one man. Curiously enough, it had bled little. He stripped off his shirt and put it around the woman, then worked the plaid shirt off the dead man and covered her waist and legs. His experienced fingers probed at the bullet wound and the woman groaned in pain. He picked her up and carried her to the edge of the trees near the stream and laid her on the soft pine needle mulch under the trees. He held her up as he put her arms into his shirt and buttoned it up the front. Then he ran back to the burned-out cabin. He found a towel on a back clothesline, wet it and brought it to her. She had no fever, but the coldness on her forehead and the back of her neck brought her closer to consciousness. She threw one arm over her eyes and mumbled some words. He wet the towel again and this time the shock of the coldness brought her eyes blinking open. They were large and brown, and they were terrified.

"Fire!" she called, but the sound was barely a whisper.

"It's all right, ma'am. The fire is almost out, you're safe now, just try to take it easy."

"The fire! And Ed!"

Her voice was stronger now. Tears sprang to her eyes, and she tried to blink them away.

"They killed my Ed. Shot him down in cold blood. They tried to kill me too . . . Chest hurts."

His fingers brushed her lips.

"Yes, don't talk, I'm a friend. Just lie still and don't talk. You've been shot. Have you spit up any blood?"

She shook her head.

"Does it hurt when you breathe deeply?"

She indicated that it didn't.

"Were you shot with a pistol?"

"Yes, from six feet."

"Strange. You really should be dead. It must have been a low powder charge or bad powder in the cartridge." He smiled. "My name is Spur McCoy, and I'm on my way to Durango. That bullet has got to come out."

"Bullet, yes." Her face suddenly reddened. She looked at the sleeve of his shirt.

"Oh, I . . . I didn't have any clothes. . . Is this your shirt?"

"Yes."

"There should be some clothes on the line in back, a dress, some . . . some underthings. I'd appreciate it."

He nodded, stood and went to the line where he'd found the towel. There were two dresses and a variety of petticoats, drawers and chemise-type garments. He took one of each and carried them back to the spot by the stream. She was sitting up.

17

"Mr. McCoy. My husband is dead, isn't he?"

"Yes."

"Rawhiders, three of them. I killed one with our Sharps. Didn't you see the body?"

"No, ma'am. They probably took it away. Some of them rawhiders have strange views about their kin and friends."

"He told Ed his name, Tom Elliott. He figured on killing Ed and me. So I shot him from inside the cabin."

"Yes, ma'am."

She sighed, looked at the clothes. "I ain't been shot before, Mr. McCoy, but I seen grown men blown six feet backwards when they get pistol shot. I just didn't feel that much force. I don't think I'm hurt bad. Would you . . ." She reddened again. "If I opened the buttons, could you look at the wound?"

"Yes, ma'am. I've had some trail experience with bullet holes."

She undid the buttons down to the third and spread the shirt. Then she unbuttoned one more and pushed back the shirt so it uncovered the wound and showed only a faint rise of her breasts. Spur sat beside her, moved her slightly so the sun shone directly on her shoulder.

His finger touched the blue-black flesh. She jumped.

"Sorry."

"No, it doesn't hurt that much. Please go on."

He had felt something strange, and then he saw why. The bluish-gray color had not been flesh at all, but the powder-blackened rear of a .44 lead slug. It had barely penetrated. He told her the situation.

"Dig it out," she said.

18

"It will hurt some."

"I know, but I'll remember how wonderful I felt when I saw that rawhider take a bullet in his heart and die. I'll talk fast and you use your knife and go under one side of it and flip it out. Don't tell me when you do it, I'll just keep talking and look the other way. Do it, Mr. McCoy! Please do it now and don't tell me when you are going to so I can keep talking and . . . *ugh*—Oh, God! Jesus Christ our Heavenly Father, have mercy on men and watch over me . . . *uuuuugh!*"

He had the wet cloth again for her head and she held it with her free hand.

"It's out, it's gone," he said. "Let me get some water and wash it. Then we'll bandage it until I can get you to a doctor."

"No. I don't want no doctor. We've got medicines . . ." She stopped and looked at the cabin. A long sigh escaped her. "There was a metal box we kept near the door that had some medicines, ointments and things. Would you take a look?"

Spur found it and used a hoe from one of the sheds to pull the hot metal box outside where it could cool off. He made another check. He found blood on the wood-pile in another section, but there was no second body. Spur found a shovel and went back to the woman

She saw him and nodded.

"Up by the spring. Ed loved that place. He could see down and across all the hundred-and-eighty acres that we were homesteading. Our third year. Two more and we would have had it proved up." She sighed and shook her head of long black hair. "We both panned for gold during the summer. They got it all . . . While you're up there, I'll get myself respectable again, have a cold bath and comb my hair . . . I don't think I even have a comb."

"I have a spare in my saddle bags, ma'am."

"Mr. McCoy. My name is Valerie Bainbridge. I'd appreciate it under the circumstances if you'd call me Valerie."

"All right, and please call me Spur."

They nodded and he went up the hill to the spring where he found a level spot and began digging a grave.

Before darkness fell that evening, Ed Bainbridge was buried. Between Spur and Valerie they salvaged many items from the burned cabin. One whole dresser drawer had not burned and she cried when she saw the clothes, including her wedding dress. A lantern in the shed still worked, and he cleared out a place for her to sleep and put down his blankets for her. He found a half loaf of bread and some baked beans that had survived the fire, and they ate that and drank coffee from his supplies. She sat watching him over the coal-oil lantern inside the six-by-eight-foot shed.

"Spur, can you use that six-gun you carry tied low on your leg?"

"Yes. I'm no fast-draw expert, but I can hit what I aim at."

"Good. Tomorrow I want you to teach me how to shoot."

"A six-gun, Valerie? A heavy Colt six-gun?"

"Whatever we have. I'm going to track down those two rawhiders and kill them."

Spur McCoy did not laugh. He watched the expression on her face, the fire in her eyes, and he knew her mind was made up. No one could talk her out of it.

"It could be dangerous."

"They shot me once, they might think I'm a ghost. I know both their first names, Mort and Chug. I'll find them, make them suffer like my Ed did, and then kill them."

"I might not have enough extra rounds for lots of target practice."

"That's no worry. Ed kept two hundred .44 rounds in here, in boxes. Should be on that first rafter."

They were, and still in the factory boxes.

"Mrs. Bainbridge . . . Valerie. I'll be honored to help you learn how to shoot. We'll start first thing tomorrow."

The metal chest was cool enough by then and Spur carried it into the shack. Some of the items inside were melted, some of the bottles broken, but she found what she wanted: arnica and carbolic. She opened the blouse she wore now and with no embarrasment dabbed the carbolic on the wound. Valerie frowned as it stung, and then redid the bandage.

"I'm not quite sure what this is, or how it works, but Ed said it was good for gunshot wounds. We'll use it and hope. I won't die of a little hole like that. It missed my collarbone and my rib, at least that was lucky." She buttoned up her blouse and looked over the other items. "Most of this will have to be thrown away." She shook her head. "It won't matter. I'm through here. I can't prove up on the place by myself, and I don't want to without Ed. Then there's a chance that Mort or Chug will be a better shot than I am, so I won't have to worry about what I do after I catch them." She turned and stared at him in such frank openness that he was surprised.

"Spur, if you can teach me how to shoot well enough, how do I go about finding these two? They said they were going to Durango."

"If you can catch them in town it will be simplist. If they get out on the trail, they'll have the advantage. And if you're on the trail you'll have to wear trousers. A skirt and petticoats are just not practical for a long trail ride."

She furrowed her brow. "I saw some of Ed's pants on the line. With some time I could cut them down so they would fit me. Take them in, shorten the legs. Pants and blouse, would that work?"

"For the trail, but the ladies would be shocked in town. So keep your dresses, or at least one, for town."

She nodded and yawned.

"Now I think it's bedtime. You sleep, you'll need it for your new life starting tomorrow." He moved to the door.

"Where are you going?"

"I'll sleep out in the woods. I'm used to it."

"Without your blankets? No. You stay here, beside me. Spur, I . . . I don't want to be alone tonight. I haven't slept alone for four years. I'm . . . I'm not inviting you even to touch me, but I'd be so grateful if you would stay." She stopped and looked at him, then blinked to hold back tears. "Spur, I'm scared to death. I'm afraid those men might come back. They . . . they raped me six times before they shot me. I'm so furious I can't even think straight. But I don't want to be here alone. Sit up if you want to or sleep beside me. Please,

22

Spur, I need help to get through this first night without my husband.''

CHAPTER THREE

An hour after Spur blew out the lantern, he was still awake. He had moved under the blanket beside her, and she had reached out to touch his back, just to make contact. She went to sleep quickly and he was pleased. She was tough, she would heal quickly, and he hoped she would give up the idea of going after the rawhiders.

She had been sleeping for a half hour when she put her arm over his chest and held on. Then she moved closer and made small sounds in her throat. She was still asleep. He reached over and kissed her cheek and she quieted. Gently he put her arm back by her side, and then slept himself.

He woke at 5:30 A.M. as he had trained himself to do. She was still sleeping. He moved from the blanket gently without waking her and looked outside. No one was there.

Spur McCoy stretched his six-foot four-inch frame and greeted the morning. He had lots of sandy red hair, a full red mustache and muttonchop sideburns. He was lean, trim and fit, and wishing the rawhiders would come back.

A telegram in his pocket was dated a week ago. It had caught up with him in Denver and was from his boss in Washington, D.C.—General Wilton D. Halleck.

PROCEED TO DURANGO COLORADO AT ONCE. SPECIAL PACKAGE TO YOU BY RAIL EXPRESS THIS DATE. DEAL WITH PROBLEM IN DURANGO OR CALL FOR AID. NO ARMY TROOPS THAT AREA AVAILABLE. CONTACT WITH ANY SALES PROBLEMS. CAPITAL INVESTIGATIONS. W.D. HALLECK. SALES MANAGER.

Another day here wouldn't hurt his job. He still hoped to talk the lady out of her mission of vengeance. It was too dangerous for her. Any rawhider was a killer by definition.

He put more rocks around the small cooking fire he had made and started boiling water for coffee. It was ready by the time Valerie came out of the shack, stretching and blinking at the sun.

She took the cup of black coffee he offered and stared into the fire. "I still can't believe that he's gone. I know I called to him last night in my sleep. I hope I didn't attack you. It was such a habit. Almost every night . . ." She broke off, her face and neck reddening.

"You make good coffee," she said.

"That will have to do for breakfast. I thought we could practice shooting here for twenty rounds, ride on toward town and stop outside a ways and practice again." He paused until she looked up. "What I was also hoping was that I could talk you out of this crazy plan.''

She shook her head. ''Spur, you can't know what it's like. You didn't have a husband of four years tortured and then shot down like he was a worthless dog. You weren't raped six times by those . . . those *animals*. You just don't know. So don't try to convince me not to do it. I am going to try, with or without your help. With your help I might be able to stay alive. You can give me a better chance.''

She changed the subject quickly.

''Do you have a needle and some thread in your saddlebags?''

He nodded, stood, and fished it out.

''A bachelor's special.''

The kit had two needles, four buttons and two small packets of flat-rolled thread. They had found a small pair of scissors in the medical kit.

''I'll get those britches stitched up right after my first six-gun lesson.'' She stood. ''Can we begin now?''

He took her to a log near the stream. Across it some twenty yards he had set up small stacks of rocks.

Spur took out his Colt and let her hold it. She almost dropped it.

''I had no idea how heavy it is! How can I ever aim it?''

''With careful training, lots of practice and by holding it in both your hands.'' He demonstrated an easy two-handed shooting stance, with both hands on the pistol grip but only one finger on the trigger.

''Now stand with your feet apart, knees slightly bent, and your elbows stiff. Now aim over the notch in the rear sight and the ridge on the front sight. Aim now.''

He let her hold it a moment.

"Now relax. It is heavy, isn't it? The more you shoot, the easier it is. Now, this time cock the hammer back with your thumb until it stops. This cocks it ready to fire, and at the same time rotates the cylinder, placing a new round in position to be fired. Clever, right? Good old Sam Colt perfected the system. Now cock the weapon." She did. "Now sight in and when you're ready to fire, squeeze your right finger against the trigger. Don't jerk it, squeeze."

She lifted the pistol, held her breath and squeezed off a shot. Three rocks that had been on top of each other disintegrated.

Spur's brows shot up. "Were you aiming at that stack?"

"Of course, Mr. Spur. Ed let me fire his pistol a little, but I really like this two-handed stance." She cocked the Colt, sighted in and blasted the second stack of egg-sized rocks. Three more shots later she was still hitting every time.

"Now reload."

He helped her take out the spent casings, and then she pushed in six fresh rounds.

"Since the modern-day pistol is sometimes prone to fire when jolted or bounced, most men carry only five live rounds in the cylinder and keep the hammer on the empty chamber for safety's sake. But since we're target practicing, I figured six rounds would let us go that much faster."

She began firing at branches, trees, at an unlucky squirrel that chattered into view. The last three shots she tried with one hand, and missed.

"That's enough for now. I think I'll stick to the two-handed stance. It really works. Now, give me a half hour to cut down those pants, and I'll be ready to ride. I'll stop outside of town and put on a skirt before we go into Durango."

"Once I get into town, I'll be busy," Spur said. "I have a job to do there that's going to take all of my time."

She frowned. "Then could we stay here another day, or move down the trail a few miles? I'd like you to show me how to get along on the trail, too."

They decided at last to stay at the cabin site one more night. She salvaged more things from the cabin. They found a horse that had been off grazing when the rawhiders were there. There was a saddle in the shack and Spur saddled the mare for Valerie, showing her exactly how to do it. Then he took the saddle off and dropped it on the ground.

"Now you saddle her," he said. "This is one job you've got to learn to do yourself."

Valerie stared at the saddle and the height of the horse, then picked up the saddle the way she had seen Spur do. At once she dropped it.

"It's so heavy!"

"True, about thirty pounds. We get to town, we'll trade for a fifteen-pound saddle, be easier for you to handle." He threw it on the horse. "Now, how do you cinch it up?" He watched her, corrected her, took it off and started again. He made her saddle the horse ten times.

"I'll *never* forget how to do that," she said wearily.

They had another shooting session and she proved to

28

be remarkably good with the six-gun at twenty and thirty feet. She had a natural feel for the weapon.

After that they found some untainted flour in the kitchen of the burned cabin, and she looked for eggs in the bushes where four white leghorn chickens scratched. She found four eggs and caught one hen, holding it by the neck and twirling it around until the head came off in her hand.

"We're going to eat tonight," she said, grabbing the flopping chicken and taking it to a pot of boiling water.

As she plucked the feathers and then cleaned the chicken, Spur tried to fill her in on trail life.

"You'll be hunting these two men. You'll have to be as tough and ruthless on the trail as they are. Never make your camp near the trail you're following. Get at least a half mile off. Don't build a fire unless you feel totally secure. Some men can smell wood smoke like this in clear mountain air from five miles away. You sleep in your clothes, including your boots, and your loaded six-gun is under your hand all the time. Trust nobody for anything, pay your way, and take no favors.

"Don't cause trouble. Mind your own business, and ask just those questions you must to keep trailing your suspect. If you spot trouble coming up, and you will because you're a beautiful woman, try to go around it. Get off the trail if you spot two or more men riding toward you. Let them go by. And never point that pistol at anyone unless you're ready, willing and anxious to shoot him dead."

She cut up the chicken with a knife that had half the handle burned off.

"When I find them, do I call them out?"

"Not unless you're tired of living. You never give a rattlesnake a fair chance if he's about to strike. You take these killers any way you can. But do it one at a time. Get one alone and use him for target practice. They didn't give your husband a chance, no fair draw. Make sure you've got the right man and then blow him into hell."

She grinned and put the chicken pot on the fire. "I think you're starting to understand how I feel."

She cut and stitched and sewed a pair of denim pants that night by the light of the lantern. Spur was getting anxious to move out. She finished the last seam and turned the pants legs right side out. She looked at them.

"I guess I should try them on."

"I'll go outside," he said.

"No, just turn your back."

He did and she struggled with the pants, lifting the petticoats out of the way. At last she had them on and buttoned up. She held up her skirts and petticoats for his inspection.

"What do you think?"

He turned. Her legs looked longer in the jeans, which clung to her softly rounded hips.

"Nice, very nice. A bit too tight, but you *are* a woman. They'll be practical on the trail. You're good with that needle."

She sat down, thanked him and didn't ask him to turn around as she unbuttoned the jeans and pulled them off. He saw the flash of her drawers, then looked away.

"We leaving early?" she asked.

"Sunup, coffee down and we're gone."

"Early to bed, then," she said. She looked at him

30

from her large brown eyes, but he read nothing there. She took off the sensible black dress shoes she had found in the rubble and hugged her knees for a moment. She watched him.

"You got a good education. What you doing out here in the mountains?"

"Working," he said. He sat there watching her. Slowly she moved toward him until her slender thigh touched his. She put her hand on his shoulder.

"Mr. McCoy, would you do me one small favor?"

He nodded.

"Would you hold me for a minute? I'm a girl who needs a man to hold her and say soft things now and then. Ed wasn't too good that way. He was a fine man, but kind of rough."

She moved against his chest and his arms went around her. She sighed softly. "Yes, that feels so good. I know I have to be mean, and vicious and unrelenting, but right now I'd rather not think about that."

She held her arms around him and tightened them. Then she spoke with her mouth against his shirt.

"Spur, would you think it wanton of me if I asked you to kiss me sweetly, just once?"

"That doesn't sound wanton to me, Valerie."

She moved and lifted her lips and met his and they kissed softly. Then she made those small noises in her throat and she kissed him harder. She moved a little so her breasts pushed directly against his chest. Their kiss ended and she murmured in pleasure. Then she lifted and kissed him again, and this time her lips were open and her tongue brushed his lips. He let her do it three times before he opened his lips and she gave a delighted

31

little sigh and pulled him gently over her as she lay down. The kiss continued. She moved her lips and whispered to him.

"Spur, I know I shouldn't, but I need you. After the way those rawhiders hurt me, I need to know that men can be soft and tender and loving. Would you help me, Spur? Help me understand how thoughtful a man can be?"

Spur had known the moment she touched him what she wanted, what she felt she must have to complete the circle, to turn the ugly sex act back into a tender and loving communion of two spirits.

He hung over her, then leaned down and kissed her lips gently.

"Whatever you want, I'll help you."

"Oh, darling, good." She kissed him and her tongue drove into his mouth, searching for some hotness to battle. Then she came away and began unbuttoning the fasteners on his shirt. Her hands brushed the soft red chest hair, then preened his mustache and his mutton-chops.

"I love red hair," she said, and kissed him again. She caught one of his hands and put it over her breast. He massaged it carefully, then found the buttons on her dress and opened them. His hand worked slowly through the fabrics until he found her bare breast.

"Yes, darling, yes!" She smiled and kissed his face as his hand toyed with her breasts.

"Darling Spur, would you get some of these clothes off me? It's getting so warm in here."

They sat up and he finished unbuttoning her dress, and she helped him lift it over her head, followed by

32

her two petticoats. Then she smiled at him. She wore a silky soft chemise over her breasts, and the leg-hugging cotton drawers. Then she undressed him: shirt, pants, underwear, right down to his skin. She was surprised by his erection.

"Oh, it's so much larger than . . ." She stopped, blushed and quickly took off her chemise. She sat up proudly, her breasts thrust forward as far as possible.

"Beautiful," he said. "A woman's breasts are her most attractive feature." He bent and kissed each and she purred, so he kissed them again.

"Spur, lay right on top of me, all the way. I want to feel your weight on top of me, holding me down."

He eased on her and felt her lithe body below him press back, mold to him, and her hips began to move slowly. Her arms came around him and pinned him to her.

"Just let me hold you this way for a while. Ed never would. Hey, you want to come back after I get rid of those two and we could settle down here and prove it up and it could be half yours and maybe we could even have a couple of kids? I always wanted two or three, but somehow we never had any."

He could see tears in her brown eyes. "No, you don't want to do that. You have a life of your own, and a job." She sniffed for a moment. "Please kiss me again, Spur, kiss me or I'm going to explode."

He kissed her and she relaxed and he rolled over so she was on top and urged her higher so he could kiss her breasts. He sucked them into his mouth and chewed tenderly and she almost climaxed.

"Wonderful! That was just wonderful," she said.

"No man ever did that so nicely." She leaned up on her elbows and looked at him. "Spur McCoy, you are one terribly nice man."

"You're just saying that because you don't have your drawers off yet."

"Oh." She paused. "I was thinking that you'd take them off when you wanted them off." She smiled. "Spur, when you found me naked and hurting and shot, what did you think?"

"I thought, here's a pretty girl in trouble who needs some help."

"But I was naked."

"True."

"Did you think I had small . . ."

"Yes, your hips are small for a girl, trim and slender and just as sexy as all hell." He lifted away from her and kissed her flat stomach, working down to the tops of the drawers. Spur undid the ties at the sides and rolled them downward. She lay there panting, then lifted on her elbows again to watch. He rolled the cotton and kissed a line across her belly, rolled it down again and kissed across and touched the first dark fringes of her pubic hair.

Valerie trembled.

He rolled the cloth down more, exposing three inches of her furry crotch, and her teeth chattered as she watched him. His head went between her legs, and she spread them and felt his lips against her wavy fur and she shivered and trembled, then roared into a moaning, shouting climax.

"Oh, damn! Again, again, *again*!" she shouted. Her flanks pounded against him; her whole body jolted and shivered and chattered as shock wave after shock wave boiled through her. She moaned in delight, her whole body quivering and jolting as one climax after another pounded through her.

At last she whimpered and reached up and kissed him and tears came to her eyes.

"So beautiful, I've never felt anything like that before. Maybe no one was gentle enough, and nobody ever kissed me . . . down there. That was so fantastic, tremendous!"

She rolled over on top of him. "Now it's your turn. I know just what to do, you lay there and relax." Her hands moved over his crotch, played with his pulled-up-tight scrotum, then touched his man-shaft. She stroked it, then bent and kissed the purple head, and his hips jolted. She kissed it again, wet it with her tongue, then kicked off her drawers and straddled his hips. She positioned herself over him, then lowered onto him, plunging his shaft deep inside her.

"Oh, heavenly. Great. God, but that's fine!" Valerie was still for a moment, working her soft bottom lower and lower against his crotch until she had engulfed every bit of his length.

Then she leaned forward and began to ride him like a pony. It had been some time, and Spur knew he would be fast. But the swarming bees slammed in on him almost at once, and his muscles tightened, his eyes bulged, and he knew it was coming. He held on as long as he could, then he pumped her high in the air as his hips pounded out a tattoo and he gave one large sigh and collapsed.

"Oh, God, you started me again!" she screeched, and

was off on another jolting pounding squealing climax that left her limp and spent and stretched on top of Spur.

She revived first, pulled away from him and lay beside him on the blanket.

"Oh, Lordy, but I will sleep tonight! I never been done so good, not ever. Not even on our wedding night when we did it seventeen times—seventeen!"

Spur put his arm around her and they pulled the blankets over them and dozed off. He woke up in the night. She was curled up hard against his side. One of her hands held his limp warrior. He wanted her again, but he shook his head. It was all right if she asked, but he didn't feel quite right demanding after what she had been through. He moved her hand, closed his eyes and went back to sleep.

CHAPTER FOUR

The next morning when Spur and Valerie were ready to leave he made her saddle her roan. The mare was a hand shorter than Spur's mount, and he made Valerie throw the saddle on by herself. At last she stood on the chopping block and heaved the saddle in place. She cinched it up and blew a strand of dark hair out of her face.

"There, I done it. In the woods I could use a stump or a fallen log, right?"

He nodded. They had found an old pistol that had been converted from percussion type loads, and she put in five rounds and a dozen more in her pocket, then dropped the six-gun into the holster and was ready to mount and leave. The gunbelt had been cut down so it fit her and rode well, low on her hip.

They followed the creek downstream to a small river, the Animas, that went right through Durango. On the near bank they picked up a faint trail of sorts. They met no one else on the trail and talked as they rode.

"Ed and me came out from Ohio. Big gold miners was our plan. We wanted to stake a claim and wound up with a homestead, but all it will support is cattle and we didn't even have a start on a herd. Ed talked about rounding up some strays, but never even got around to that. We went to Denver once. What a long trip! Ed had big plans, just not much ever came of them. What about you? Bet you went to college and everything."

Spur grinned. "Yes, I went to college, and worked as an aide to a U.S. senator in Washington D.C. and even put in my time in the Army in the big war."

"And now you're a marshal or something?" she asked, her eyes bright.

"I work with Capital Investigations, a kind of detective agency."

"Like the Pinkertons?"

"Only we're better than the Pinkertons. We don't compete with them."

"And you're going to Durango on some problem. Bet somebody killed somebody." She quieted and rode a few hundred feet thinking. "If it don't work out that I can kill these guys, could I hire you to run them down?"

"Not to kill them. I'd have to arrest them for trial."

"But I was all alone. Be just my word against theirs. And they would claim I made it all up . . . Well, then I guess we better stop somewhere and let me sharpen up my shooting eye. I got me a pair of men to shoot full of holes."

She did not smile when she said it.

They did stop once more, well out of Durango, and

she showed him how she could pick rocks off stumps at forty feet.

"Don't try a shot any farther than that, even two-handed. These weapons aren't made for it. Fifteen or twenty feet is lots better."

On the rest of the ride, he taught her a little bit about tracking, how to pick out one hoofprint or shoe print from a group, how to determine the condition of the horse, how a heavy print could mean riding double on one horse.

With all the backtracking, teaching and meandering, they rode into Durango just before noon. Durango was still a rough little mining town, with a few stabs at respectability and a thin gloss over some of the rougher elements. But mining still made it run and supplying the mines and the miners was the biggest business in town.

Valerie had put a dress on over her blouse and pants a mile out of town, and rode in primly sidesaddle, one leg hooked around the horn and feeling cramped and uncomfortable. But she was smiling when Spur helped her down at the Mountain Lodge Hotel. Spur took their horses to the livery a block away, then came back and registered himself. As he did he saw she had signed in as Amy Bostwick, her middle and maiden names. She was in 202. He took the key to room 210 and went up the steps, his saddlebags and carpetbag in tow. The room was spartan, with a wooden floor, one window with a shade and no curtain. The bedstead was of iron and the bedsprings almost nonexistent. There was a small dresser with a wavy-lined mirror over it and a wash-stand, but no pitcher of water or wash basin. He was spoiled, and this was the best hotel in town.

Spur opened his carpetbag and took out the big brown envelope, pulled the papers from inside it and sat on the bed reading. He had been through most of it before, but a refresher wouldn't hurt.

His assignment was a trio of counterfeiters. Counterfeiting had been the primary job of the Secret Service when it was started back in 1865. There had been a sudden flurry of high quality twenty-dollar bills flooding Denver lately and the trio of sharpies had been traced to Durango. But none of the phony money had surfaced there. He nodded. That made sense—don't foul your own nest.

There were notes about one of the three, a woman, a gifted artist who was the platemaker, the engraver, for the team. She had sold several paintings before moving into her current line of work. Nothing was known of the other two except one was a black man. Spur finished reading the stack of papers, looked at pictures of the bad bills and paid special attention to some of the mistakes on them. Then he went to the desk downstairs and ordered a pitcher of hot water and a basin sent up to his room.

After a good scrubbing of his face and torso, Spur put on a fresh cotton flannel plaid shirt and clean black pants. He polished up his boots and took a tour of the town. There were still more saloons, gambling halls and whorehouses in Durango than all the rest of the businesses put together. Spur had a half-chilled beer at the first saloon and listened to the talk. Horses, guns, mining and a little about cattle. Nothing that would do him any good. he watched a poker game for a while and saw a man who obviously was a miner lose over two hundred dollars. That was as much as the miner would make in six months working in the mines.

Spur had a bowl of stew and biscuits at a small restaurant down the street and had to pay fifty cents for it. He was surprised. He had forgotten that everything had to be hauled in. That made it cost more.

He picked up a copy of the local newspaper, the Durango *News*. There wasn't much in it: two shootouts on Main Street, one man slightly wounded, nobody hit in the other one. A killing in back of a mining dormitory hall, and the town's favorite dog, "Floppy," was pregnant again.

Spur leaned against a hotel wall for a while, letting the afternoon sunshine warm him. Then he sat in a straight-backed chair and tipped it up against the hotel. It was a good afternoon for a quick nap.

But his mind was whirling. He'd never come on a case with so little to go on. Not even a name. A woman and a black man in the trio. They might not be so hard to find after all. He had no idea how many people in Durango, maybe a thousand, two thousand in the whole area. He needed to know more about the town. He snapped his fingers. Newcomers. This pair would have come into town during the past two or three months. Yes, he was narrowing it down. But who could he talk to? Who would be prudent enough? Probably not the sheriff, if they had one. He would be owned by the mining interests, hog barrel and pork swill. Who else in town would know nearly everyone? The general store merchant, maybe a preacher, maybe the newspaper editor. He lifted his brows. This counterfeiting operation called for an elaborate printing press, a good

41

flatbed that could hold a fine line registration for the color work. Where better than a newspaper?

He strolled down the walk to the false front labeled *La Plata County Sheriff's Office and Jail. La Plata*—"the silver" from the Spanish. There was certainly enough silver around Durango, from what Spur had heard.

The sheriff's office was next to the county assessor's office. He went in and saw a connecting door into a series of barred cells. No one was in the outer office.

Spur usually made it a policy to check out the sheriff anywhere that he would be operating. He could pull rank on him later if he needed to, and he wanted to know what kind of a lawman held power. He always worked with the officials if he thought they were honest. As a U.S. Secret Service agent he found the local police could often help.

A moment after the door closed behind Spur, a man rolled into the room walking with the easy grace of a man long used to the uneven and undulating boards of a ship at sea. He was middle-sized, with a three-inch red scar on his forehead, and looked dressed more for the open country than town with his red bandana over a blue shirt, soft leather vest with latigo-type ties, and a pair of blue denim pants covering worn and scuffed cowboy boots.

"Afternoon!" the man said with a grin. Spur figured he was midway through his forties.

"Well, a good afternoon right back to you. You the sheriff?"

The man chuckled, shifted a wad of tobacco in his mouth and shook his head. "Not likely. Sheriff Hanshoe ain't here right now. His full monicker is Amos P. Hanshoe, but he's out.''

Spur liked and trusted this man at once. ''I figure anything I wanted to talk about with the sheriff I can say to you. Man of your talents must be valuable around here. Your mama give you a name?''

The other man chuckled again. '' 'Pears as how. But I never use it. You can call me Cyrus, Cyrus Mercer.''

Spur pushed out his hand. ''Spur McCoy. I do some work in these parts for an outfit called Capital Investigations, kind of half-assed detective work. Looking for some folks, and figured you might remember some new people in town that fit their descriptions.''

Cyrus shifted the chaw again, spit at a hidden spittoon and then peered up, squinting out of one eye.

''Nigh onto two thousand folks hereabouts now, Mr. McCoy. Danged if I know half of them even by eyeball.''

''How it be if I bought you a beer and we can talk about it?''

''Don't see why not, an afternoon brew never did bother my constitution none. Right next door is the Laughing Lady saloon. I'll just lock the front door here and take me a small siesta.''

In the just-opened saloon they had mugs of nickle beer and settled down at a table near the back. Spur sat so he faced the door. The beer was half cold and not bad.

''Cyrus, you call me Spur, right? Now, this pair I'm looking for makes an odd couple. The woman is tall, maybe five-ten or five-eleven. Stands out in a crowd. She's about thirty, maybe thirty-five and is something of an artist. The man, on the other hand is a black, five-eight, lots of scars on his back from his slave days, and

43

I've heard he's a fair man at the printing trades."

Cyrus began to grin. "Damn fine beer they got here, know that? I told old Mandy last week he served the best glass in town." Cyrus took another long pull at the glass and wiped the foam off his mouth.

Spur nodded. "No rush, Cyrus. Have another brew. I got me all day. How long they been in town?"

"Maybe three months. You described them to a fare-thee-well. Woman calls herself Kathleen Smith. Gettin' to be too dang many Smiths around here for my taste. She's tall and solid and she does do some sketching stuff. She also came in and bought out the local newspaper, the Durango weekly *News.*"

"Runs the paper? Well, that's a switch for her. Nothing I can tell you right now, like she isn't wanted for murder or anything. More of a tracer we got hired to make. I don't know if it's an angry husband or what. I just follow orders."

Spur signaled for another pair of beers, paid for them, and Cyrus grinned. "Pay pretty good for detective kind of work?"

"Fair. At least I get to do a lot of traveling. You looking for work?"

Cyrus cast a sky-blue-eyed look at Spur and chuckled. "Not likely. I damned well put together this town, such as it is. I was the first town marshal back fifteen years ago. For a mining town to live fifteen years is a damn miracle."

"And you been mother-henning Durango ever since."

"Yep, like my firstborn, if I had one. You don't want me making no chin music to the sheriff about our talk?"

"True enough, Cyrus. Another beer?"

"Spur, you not supposed to get me drunk, just ply me a little." Cyrus shook his head. "Nope. Got to get back and mind the store. One prisoner is there, but he's just a drunk sleeping it off. Still, never can tell."

Spur held out his hand. "Been a pleasure meeting you, Cyrus Mercer. I'll be around for a while. We'll have to talk about old times again."

Cyrus took the hand and nodded, his blue eyes friendly, satisfied with his world.

"See you, Spur. Tread careful in this town. Hear?"

Spur nodded and walked out of the saloon into the afternoon sun. He went across the street past the general store and a new-looking haberdashery to a small storefront with a sign over top that read: *The Durango Weekly News*. He pushed open the door and stepped inside.

The musty, undeniable smell of paper hit him. It was the one smell that every newspaper office in the world had. The musty, cheap, one-time use paper in large pasteboard boxes was just waiting to be marked with print.

A tall woman behind the waist-high counter looked up, her serious expression giving way to a reluctant smile.

"Yes?"

"I'd like to see the publisher, please."

"I'm the publisher." She laughed softly. "The publisher, the printer's devil, the editor, the janitor, the bookkeeper, the advertising salesman and often the delivery man. What can I do for you?"

It was Spur's turn to smile. She was a big woman, a

45

good five-eleven, with proportionate shoulders and large heavy breasts to fit her size. Her torso tapered sharply toward her waist. She wore a high-necked soft blue dress and had brown hair cut severely short. Her glance went over him as he looked at her.

"Could I buy a copy of this week's paper? I'm looking for property and thought there might be some ads of things for sale, the way there are in the papers back east."

She handed him a copy and smiled. "Compliments of the new mangement."

"New?"

"We've only been here three months, it still feels new. Where in the east do you hail from?"

"Missouri, Ohio. Lived for a while in New York."

"I want to get there someday." She turned away, then looked back. "You need any help, just ask. I've got to get this advertisement drawn up or I'll get shot by our printer."

Spur looked through the advertising section. There were two houses for sale, one business, lots of horses and used mining equipment. He read part of the front page, folded it, and tucked it under his arm.

"A nice little paper," he said.

"Thank you, we try. Find anything you like?"

Spur almost swallowed his mustache. She had turned so her breasts thrust at him and she was now closer, well within touching distance. He controlled his face and shook his head.

"Nothing in my price range. I'll put a notice on the public bulletin board by the general store. If that doesn't work, I'll run one of your ads for

46

building wanted.''

"I hope you do, we can always use the business." She moved sharply and her breasts jiggled through the tightness of the dress.

"About prices . . . Sometimes I discover in this town that things are not nearly as expensive as they first seem. There's always plenty of time for bargaining.'' She smiled, her double meaning coming at him as plain as a three-dollar bill.

Spur smiled and tilted back his low-crowned gray Stetson.

"Well now, I always do like to bargain. I'm obliged to you for the advice and kind words.'' He smiled. "Thanks for the paper, too." He turned and walked out the newspaper-office door, knowing that she watched him leave.

CHAPTER FIVE

Kathleen Smith watched Spur leave and when the door closed she expelled a large breath. Her brown eyes danced as she followed his smooth hip action as he crossed the street.

Damn, but he was pretty! she thought. How in hell could she have made it any plainer that she was interested? Sure, she could have ripped open her bodice. She smiled and went back to work on the advertisement she was putting together.

Henry parted the curtain and came into the front office. He wore an inky printer's apron with a dozen pockets in it. He was a black man who had survived the slave ships when he was a boy and had endured much more since then. His back was laced with scars from an overseer's whip. Henry was three inches shorter than Kathleen and slender.

"I'm working on it, Henry."

"Yes, I see. But not half as hard as you worked on

that dude in the gray Stetson."

Anger flamed her face for a moment, but then she laughed.

"Henry, you're an ugly nigger, you know that? I'll have this done in a minute."

"Yassuh, boss lady. Yassuh! You shore will," he said, dropping into field-style uneducated black talk.

"Fuck you, Henry," she said, still grinning.

"You done it before, probably happen again," he said. When he spoke next it was with a clipped, precise English accent. "I am waiting for the copy, Mrs. Smith."

She waved at him and bent over the stand-up desk.

Two mintues later she had it finished and carried the rough layout to the print shop. No one else was there. She handed the paper to Henry and put her hand on his shoulder.

"Hey, I've got an itch in a place I can't scratch."

"Can't or don't want to?" he said, his hands working over a drawer holding a font of headline type.

"You know which one, Henry." She caught his hand and pulled it against her breasts. "Come on, Henry, don't tease me."

He looked around the shop. "Christ, just what you did now would a been plenty to get me shot ten years ago."

"You're not a slave now, Henry, remember that. Just close your eyes and pretend I'm one of those big, hot, black mamas you said you used to do stud service on."

"I told you that?"

"Late one night you told me, after I had you a little drunk and all sexed up."

He unbuttoned the fasteners on the front of her dress

and pushed one black hand inside and under the chemise. Henry chuckled.

"Damn, but you got the tits. I always said that. Big and firm and hot, like two volcanos ready to erupt."

"Don't talk so much, Henry."

She pulled the front of the dress open farther, pushed down her two petticoats and the chemise and lifted one big breast into the open.

"Oh, God!" Henry said. He bent and kissed the mountain, then pulled half of it into his mouth and sucked and chewed the enlarged nipple.

The front door opened and closed.

"Christ!" she said. She pushed him away, popped her breast back into the dress and began furiously buttoning it up. A few moments later she called out.

"Just a moment, I'll be right there." She finished with the dress, picked up a stick of type and walked into the front office.

Henry listened from the curtain. Somebody wanted a story in the *News* that her daughter was getting married. Henry watched through the curtain. Kathleen was standing on one foot, then the other. She was needing to be poked again. Maybe after they got the paper run off. She'd be tired by then, maybe he could keep up with her. Henry grinned.

"Thank you, President Lincoln," he said softly. "Thank you just one hell of a lot!"

As they put the final sticks of type into place and Kathleen checked the proof sheet Henry pulled, they talked quietly about the other part of their business.

"So as long as we come out with a small paper, it

50

gives us a perfect camouflage. Who would suspect, right? And I'm working on the new plates. Our contact has left Denver and moved to New Orleans. We'll start sending him a few bills in letters by courier and stage as soon as we get them finished. If they look good we get a big order and we should be able to close up and get out of here before anybody finds us."

"What about pretty boy, the gray Stetson? His story about a building sounded phony as hell to me." Henry stared at her.

"Oh? I didn't notice. To me it sounded reasonable."

"That's because, woman, you was thinking with your crotch. I got a big stake in this game, remember? Sure, we both have nice bank accounts in Denver, but they ain't gonna do us no good if they slam us into a federal prison somewhere."

"Nobody is going to get caught. We're too good for that, Henry. Three years we been working, right? The average outfit lasts about three months after the first bills hit circulation. It will work again for us."

Henry shrugged. "Yassuh, boss lady. Whatever you say."

She laughed at his slave-boy lingo. "Damn right, nigger. Now let's get this newspaper put out and get on with the important stuff. We've still got a hundred thousand dollars worth of those Denver twenties to print."

Late that night, before they were done with the 400 copies of the little four-page paper, a man walked in the back door, sucked on a small flask of whiskey and stared at them. He was unkempt, older than he looked, with a full beard and mustache that hadn't been trimmed in several months. His eyes showed as red-rimmed circles. A smirk covered his face.

"Yeah, like to see you guys working. Gonna work all fucking night?"

"Watch your language!" Henry barked at him.

"So make me, black boy."

Kathleen left her work folding the printed papers and went to where the man stood.

Pat O'Reilly watched her coming. What a big bitch of a woman. But right then he didn't give a damn. They had promised him a lot of action. Hell, he hadn't lifted a finger in three months. Then she was beside him. He sniffed the faint touch of perfume.

"Patrick, love, what's the matter? Ain't them cathouse girls good enough for you? Ain't you getting enough?"

He snorted. She always could twist him around. He couldn't help but look at the blouse she wore which she must have opened another button on as she walked over. He could see the bulging tops of both of her big breasts. Goddamn! He reached for them. She pushed his hand away.

"Patrick, like I told you before. You have your job, we have ours. Any time you want to cut out for a richer vein or a better job, you just cash in your chips and move on. You can get out of our game any time. And like I told you, I don't sleep with pigs. You get a bath and a haircut and trim your fucking beard and buy yourself some new clothes, and we'll tussle any time you say."

Henry came up wiping grease off his hands. "I still think I smell a rat in that tall man who came this afternoon."

Pat's eyes came alive. "Trouble?"

"Could be," Henry said. "He's tall, six-two, about thirty, wears a low-crowned gray Stetson. He's got the look and the feel of a gentleman, somebody who is just playing with us."

Pat snorted. "He came in once and you know all that? Wait until Katy here gets into his bed."

She slapped him gently. "I ain't asked him yet."

"Find out where he stays," Henry said. "We just might want you to visit him late some night and chop his head off."

Pat's face roiled in sudden anger.

"I got to take orders from a nigger?"

"Nobody gives orders, Pat. You know that," Kathleen said.

"We suggest what needs to be done and decide. We're even partners three ways around. Now if you don't want to do your job, you don't get your cut, an—"

Pat held up his hand. "Just funnin' you-all. Christ!"

"Yassuh, boss. This old nigger, he just mosey back to the little old press and make it turn out money for you-all white folks to spend."

He went back to the press and Kathleen wasn't sure if Henry's lingo was all in fun.

"Don't mess with Henry," she said softly. "Without him we are back to hustling drinks and picking pockets."

"It's a good, hard-working living."

"I like this one better. Keep tabs on the tall stranger. If he shows any sign that he's a U.S. Marshal, you know what to do with no directions from us."

O'Reilly brightened. "Yeah, I'll just do that. I'll stick with that dude like a mud plaster."

"And in the meantime, get a bath and a haircut, or he'll spot you right off."

"Yeah, I'll do it. Damn, what tits!" He reached out again and this time she didn't move. He wormed one hand inside her blouse around the swell of the orb and he swore softly. "Almost be worth getting a fucking bath for."

She pushed his hand away. "Remember how good that felt, Pat, and go take a bath."

He shrugged, tipped the whiskey flask again, and then went out the back door.

An hour later the press stopped rolling. Henry had hand fed the last of the big sheets into the flatbed double crank and foot lever actuated press. Kathleen looked up.

"Done?"

"Four hundred. Wish to hell they was all sheets of twenty dollar bills."

"They will be the next time. We should get in a money press run this week. So it will be blackout time again."

He stood beside her. "I could help you fold the rest of those." He hesitated, then bent in and kissed the hollow between the large breasts.

"Or we could do it in the morning?" she said.

54

Her hands stopped moving. She swallowed. His mouth pushed at the fabric over her breasts. Her hand came up and opened the buttons and pulled down the cloth.

Henry rumbled in his throat as his lips closed around her breast, nibbling at the already erect nipple. He turned her, chewed lightly on her again, then looked up. "You been hot for a good one all day. Damn near teased old Pat into jumping you, so right now let's you and me find that cot of yours in back."

"Henry, before it's been when *I* wanted to."

"Yeah, and that's what bothers me. It ain't fair. We ain't real partners that way. This time I want to, so why not? Fair is fair."

She nodded. "Yeah, I guess." Kathleen Smith unbuttoned the last fasteners on her blouse, pulled it off her shoulders and dropped it on the floor. Then she tugged down at her petticoats and the chemise.

"Henry, you're a printer, right? You ever made love to anyone on the goddamned flatbed press?"

He laughed, rubbing the erection showing behind his fly.

"I sure ain't as hell ever have, but I bet you neither one of us gonna be able to claim that tomorrow!"

He chuckled as he chewed on both her bare breasts. "Shit, you gonna get printing ink all over your bare ass!"

"Or maybe on my dress, or some cardboard. What about that newsprint box all flattened out?"

It was in place a minute later and she had opened his pants. His male staff surged outward, so dark and black, so wicked! Christ, but her father would die all over again if he could see her now. She grabbed the stiff rod and pulled him toward her.

"Easy!" Henry said. "This time I call the shots, and the speed and the pace and the fucking positions. You just play at being a nice little girl."

She shrugged, felt his hands on both her breasts. Now the heat was building. She could sense her breasts bursting into flames, feel her crotch twitching. He sucked on her breasts again and asked her to bend over so they hung like two giant bells, with his mouth and teeth devouring both.

"Henry, tell me something true."

"Sure."

"You get a special thrill out of fucking a white girl?"

He shook his head. "Back before the war the white girls all thought we did. I was about sixteen and this little white girl from the big house was fourteen. She wanted me the worst way. Always found a way to get me alone in the woods. But I never more than played with her titties. I knew damn well if I fucked her, she'd scream rape and I'd be hung inside of an hour. I done stud work for three years. A woman is a woman—a big black mama with massive breasts, or a little scared fifteen-year-old virgin with almost no tits at all."

"And me, Henry?"

"You got tits like I never seen before. Big suckers, but firm and almost no sag. Damn white mountains. But is white ass different? Maybe a little extra thrill 'cause I know the Southern whites even in this town would lynch me quick they found me with my cock inside you.''

She pushed him back and pulled the dress and petticoats off over her head. He undid the chemise and now she wore only knee-length trousers made of soft, thin cotton. He stared at them.

"Bloomers," she said. "Least they were, but they were long and gathered around the ankles. I cut them off. Sort of underpants.''

He laughed and pulled off his shirt and then his pants and stood in front of her, blackly naked.

She trembled. "Oh, God, Henry, but you're so black!''

"And you're so ghost white. You still want to?''

She closed her eyes. "Yes! Oh, God, yes! Hold me.''

His arms went around her, and her big breasts flattened against his chest as she felt his warm skin against hers, and it didn't seem black at all. She rubbed his back with her hands and felt the warm skin. A man! Right then she didn't care what color he was or who he was as long as he was there! He was black. It did give her a little added thrill knowing she was violating the traditions of the South and her own family. She felt a hot burning in her that she wasn't sure would ever go out.

His hands were so gentle, soft, exploring—a youth's hands finding a new universe of fleshly pleasure. They feathered over her back with the delicacy of a blind man's talented touch upon his friend or lover. His touch fully consumed her last shreds of doubt and worry, and quickly she knew she could not deny him anything he wanted.

Her body suddenly squirmed against the smaller,

harder one in front of her. His erection pushed against her belly and she whimpered in expectation.

"I'm gonna take you, big woman, I'm gonna flatten you out on that flatbed press and give you exactly what you want." Henry's words came in whispers close to her ear. He chewed at her earlobe and it sent Kathleen into a shivering spell that surprised even her.

"Don't stop!" she whispered huskily. "Whatever the fuck you're doing, don't stop it."

He let some space come between their bodies and one of his hands came up to claim a mountainous breast. She knew she was burning him but she didn't care. She *wanted* to burn him, to love him.

"Henry, talk dirty to me, I love it."

His lips chewed on her ear again and she squirmed, wishing she had the bloomers off, wishing her whole naked body could press against his whole naked body.

"Katie, sweetheart, you gonna get fucked, you know that. I'm gonna spread you out on that press and stick my cock into you. My big, black cock into your soft, sweet, white little pussy. You want it, don't you? You get a wild thrill doing something your old pappy would whip you silly for. Black meat, you gonna get some black meat into your white-ass little cunt hole and you gonna love it!"

She pushed away from him and pulled down the bloomers, kicking them off her feet, pulling his hand into her crotch.

"Damn, we can't do anything standing up," she said. She stepped up to the flatbed of the press. "Will it hold both of us?"

"Should," he said. "If it don't, what a way to break a press!"

She grinned, sat down on the cardboard and pushed herself back until she could lie down.

"Hey, I ain't no whore, you ain't even kissed me yet."

He came over her like a black avenger, pushed her spread knees together and lay full and heavy on top of her. Then his mouth reached for hers, her eyes closed, and his tongue forced its way into her mouth.

For just a moment she felt a lurch as she realized a black tongue was in *her* mouth and a black man lay naked and sexed up and ready to fuck on top of *her* naked body. Then she slammed the door on her parents, pushed them back into their own era with their mores and taboos, and welcomed the tongue, fought it and tried to batter it back out of her mouth. She did and then her tongue darted into his moist hot cavity and she heard him moan in pleasure and his hips began pushing slowly against hers. But he'd pinned her legs together with his knees.

She pumped her damp loins upward anyway, trying to make contact with his manhood, but couldn't. She forced the heat of her crotch into his undulating flesh and her furry nest bristled against him, searching for its own fulfillment.

Over her, Henry knew she was ready and so was he, but he was in no hurry. He could tease her, heat her up for a half hour yet and get her on the edge of her own satisfaction even before he entered her. It was a little like his early years, when his master had trained him to be a stud. The young master had made him sit and watch while he put his white meat into the young, pretty mulatto girls, and Henry was supposed to learn. Then his master sat and watched the sixteen-year-old do it, always with the man on top because that was the best for getting the bitch pregnant. He shook his head and looked down at the soft white face and the short brown hair of Kathleen Smith. He'd come a long way in a few years.

He kissed her again and their tongues tangled; hers slithered between his lips and they battled again, his one hand firmly around her left breast, and he could feel the nipple throbbing in his palm.

The whole world was blazing again, fired by the ancient emotions created even before man was black or white or yellow. The earth exploded and dazzled the burning sun. She tried to turn over, but he shook his head indicating there was no room. He lifted up and stared down at her, at her big tits, flattened now by her position, and her skin glistening with the mingled sweat from their throbbing bodies. He looked at the soft brown fur thatch between her legs and he shivered just thinking about probing into the depths of her hidden place. She grabbed his prick and pulled it down. Then her knees opened, legs spread, and her hips pushed up toward him, thrusting the heart of her in the ancient invitation of the drive to reproduce.

Henry wiped sweat from his face, kissed her once more and moved down to her white peaks, chewing on her nipples, giving her one last moment to think about it.

Then he moved, knelt between her thighs and spread her inner leg more with his fingers, parting the thatch, opening the love lips as he adjusted himself. He suddenly drove forward and down in a surge that sunk him deeply into her quivering sheath.

Her sharp cry could be heard in the street. It was an explosion of joy and surprise, of the unending desire to be loved and bred and needed, and the rapture of a man's stiff penis inside her to scratch that itch that had been tormenting her. He pushed farther and farther into the satin folds of her heartland and she grabbed him with those special muscles and held him a moment, sending quivering shocks up his stem and almost making him climax. Then she let him go, pulsing, squeezing him now and then to give him an added thrill.

"Beautiful!" he said. "So damn beautiful!" The words rolled out of his mouth without his fully understanding that he said them. Came out as if saved for a special occasion not to be wasted.

Kathleen had her arms firmly around his back. Her eyes were tightly closed and her mouth gasped for breath. She knew it was coming, and so fast. She knew she would explode into a billion particles in just a few moments and never be put back together again.

The first sign came with a tingling in her arms and then her toes, then her whole nervous system jangled as if some electrode had sent sparks of electricity against her raw nerve endings in a million places in her body, and they all responded with pain and pleasure at once.

She jerked, she vibrated—for one moment she

thought she might be dying—then the spasms shook her, one after another, multiplying, building, surging higher and higher until she felt so shaken and rattled that she would fall into pieces. The vibrations hit her again and again as she let out all of her frustrations and angers, all of her futile search for a man tall enough for her. She shook and panted and rolled under him but he never came out. She danced and pawed and clawed his back, and her voice was on constant high, wailing and moaning softly, then panting, and at the end whispering soft words of endearment.

He rode through it with her, then stroked twice and felt how deep he could go and realized she was a big woman and he couldn't halfway fill her, but he tried.

Her climax had lit up his senses like a burning cotton shed. His own body had reacted to her cries and her moans and especially the whispers.

And then he couldn't hold back.

He took her. He had his way with her. He drove into her like a raging stallion, like a range bull too long from the herd. He plowed and pounded and built to the heights of ecstasy. Henry was surprised at her continued reactions. She cried, then gasped, clutched and again clawed at him as his own passions built and his flesh ground against hers. He filled her completely now.

Some part of his self-worth came roaring back, some part of his early bad life balanced out. The worst times were eased and clouded over so they didn't hurt so much with the knowledge that he could satisfy this big woman on even terms, that he was a *man* again and not just a black slave.

He sailed her over the moon. He made her fly like an eagle, soaring from mountain to mountain, cruising down the valleys of pleasure, through the soft, gentle woodlands, past rushing streams, along everything that is good and wonderful and valid.

Then he exploded.

There was no more holding back and he was aware even as he drove into her hard and sure and with finality that he triggered her again and she bucked and swayed and spasmed under him, her fingernails raking down his scarred back. He knew he was calling her name again and again as he emptied his seed into her infertile field. And suddenly they were kissing again, their lips bruised, and then he tasted his own blood as her teeth crushed one small bit of his flesh and blood mingled with salty sweat dripping off their faces.

At last they both relaxed; the kiss ended and his chin hooked over her shoulder.

Neither of them spoke for some minutes. Then she moved. He lifted off her, stepped off the press and helped her to sit up.

"My God!" she said. "Screwed on a flatbed press! I still don't believe it. Best impression you ever made, Henry!"

He grinned. Then he knew she wanted him gone. He picked up his clothes and vanished into the back, darker area of the big room. They both dressed quickly, locked the back door and walked to the small house she had purchased when they arrived. Then he went around back to the small barn and his bunk in the loft.

Henry grinned as he lay on his back on the bunk. Oh, but it had been sweet, and he *had* lied to her. Yes, he did get an added thrill each time he fucked a white woman. It was one more "get back" at that damn white man with the whip. He could never get even, but at least he would try!

CHAPTER SIX

When Valerie Bainbridge had registered in room 202 of the Mountain Lodge Hotel, she had used Amy Bostwick. her middle and maiden names, but only as a safety precaution. The men who had raped her had heard her first name and they might—just might—check the hotel registers if they thought she could have followed them.

She thought only for a moment about the large man who had rescued her—probably saved her life—and taught her what she needed to know. Now she had a mission, a vengeance to satisfy. She began that same afternoon. She had a bath first, then put on one of her dresses that hadn't burned and checked the hotel registers around town. There were four. She said she was hunting her brother and his friend. She was supposed to meet them here but they hadn't contacted her yet.

The hotel clerks, mostly young men, had been more than helpful. At the third hotel they found both names listed for one room.

"Here they are. Chug Rollins and Mort Sawtell," the clerk said at the Montana Hotel.

She smiled sweetly at him. She hadn't forgotten how to do that. "Thank you. You've been most helpful. I want to surprise them, so don't tell them we talked. All right?"

Her smile was so pretty, so sweet, that the clerk nodded at once. She had the room number in her mind, 111 on the ground floor. Already she was making plans. She went to the side of the hotel, a small, two-story building with not over twenty rooms altogether, and looked down the alley. There was one house behind it, more than a hundred feet on the street beyond. No other stores, and plenty of places to drift off into the landscape. Yes, that was good.

Valerie walked slowly back to her hotel. It was two blocks and all the way she was thinking. Trying to remember everything Spur McCoy had told her about the gun, about shooting a man face to face. She was tough enough to do it. She was still sore from the pounding they had given her. And they had shot Ed down without giving him a chance and made him suffer horribly as well. Yes, dammit, she *could* shoot them!

She went past the desk and up the stairs, wearing a grim expression that she realized she would have to get rid of. She was a sweet little lady who couldn't possibly do anything like shoot a man down.

In her room, Valerie checked over her appearance in the wavy mirror. Her long black hair was partly covered by a small dark hat and she had on a nondescript brown gingham dress that swept the ground properly. She decided to change her hat, and then she found the

66

only reticule she had left, a small one, not large enough for the pistol. It was an old Colt that had been converted from percussion caps to solid cartridges. She took it out and checked all six cylinders. She had loaded five and the hammer was on the empty one. She tried holding the weapon behind a shawl, but that was awkward—surely someone would notice. She was not even sure when the best time would be to find the men in their room. Two of them. Gingerly she opened the pistol and loaded another round into the empty chamber. That would be three rounds for each man.

Valerie tried the six-gun in her reticule again. Then she took everything out of it and pushed the Colt in muzzle first. By holding the gun in the bag with the top extended, she could conceal it, and by sliding her hand inside the bag she could catch hold of the butt trigger and fire right through the reticule if she had to.

Yes, it would work!

She took her father's big pocket watch out of her carpetbag. It was just after three o'clock. Perhaps they would be in their room. If so, it would be simple. Of course she would have to get away after she shot them.

Valerie grabbed her purse-like reticule and went out her door. She locked the room and moved quickly down the hall.

At first the big six-gun was heavy, awkward, but the more she carried it, the easier it became. She caught it with her left hand, slid her right inside the reticule, gripped the handle and slid her finger onto the trigger. Yes, up close she could fire it one-handed. What she must not do was grab the cylinder with her left hand, even through the cloth. That would stop the weapon

67

from firing. Spur had been emphatic about that point.

She moved the reticule, carrying it with both hands now, her right still on the handle of the .44. Her modified sunbonnet hid most of her face and all of her hair. She walked on the far side of the street from the hotel, crossed over and went along the side street to the back entrance of the Montana Hotel. Number 111 was three doors in. No one was in that end of the hall. She knocked.

Silence from inside. It had been too easy.

She knocked again. Still no one was in the hall. This time she heard a groan from inside the room, listened to a bed squeak and then heard soft footfalls coming toward the door. She had draped a thin veil over the top of the sunbonnet and now she lowered it to help disguise her features from the killers.

The key turned in the lock.

As the door opened the voice inside growled.

"Mort, what the hell you doing coming back here, I thought . . ."

Chug Rollins stopped when he saw the woman. He took a step back and stared at her.

"Miss, you got the wrong room," he said, still blinking.

"No, this is one-eleven, isn't it? The girls said I should come over and thank you in just any way I could. They appreciate all your business last couple of days."

"Huh? Them whores don't give away nothing."

"We are this time. I'm new and it's my introduction to the town. I figure I let you men know what I got, they gonna like me more."

"Yeah? No shit?" He rubbed his chin.

"Well, we better close the door. I advertise but not out here in the hallway." She stepped inside and shut the door.

"Now, let me get this straight," Chug said, backing up. He caught a bottle off the dresser and sat down on the bed. He took a drink from it and squinted up at her. "You mean you gonna give me a free one, an afternoon fuck right here in my own room?"

"It's what we call our delivery service," Valerie said. He wore no shirt, just his pants. "Only thing you need to do is strip for action, then I get ready."

"Hell, no problem there." He unhooked his belt and let his pants fall. He wore no underwear. His manhood was soft and drooping. Chug stared at her. "You must a been there last couple of nights. Swear I seen you before, even through that veil."

"Doubt it. They say you're called Chug."

"Right." He kicked his pants off and stood watching her.

"Good, Chug Rollins, because my name is Valerie, and I'm here to kill you." She pulled the Colt from her reticule, letting the bag fall to the floor. She grabbed the weapon in her usual two-handed stance and cocked it.

He laughed and moved slowly toward her.

"Shit, you don't even know how to hold that thing! You ain't gonna shoot nobody. And I'm—"

She aimed low at his belly and fired. The shot went lower still, nicking his flaccid penis, tearing solidly into the right side of his scrotum, splattering into a hundred wet smears the testicle hanging there, and froze Chug in his stride. Then he jolted backwards, his scream shattering the room.

She moved toward him quickly, knowing there wasn't much time. Because of the warm day Chug had opened the window that morning, and she saw it hanging open. Valerie walked up to Chug, who lay on the floor by the bed, his hands tenderly holding his mangled genitals.

"I'm Valerie Bainbridge, the woman you raped three times and then shot in the chest and left for dead in a burning cabin. Remember?"

"Christ, I'm *dying*," he choked. "Help me. For God sake, *help me!*"

"The same way you helped Ed, my husband, when you shot him? Fine, I'll help you that way." She shot his right knee, pulverizing it, rolling him over on the wooden floor. "I'll help you some more, Chug." She shot him again in the crotch, the bullet blasting through his hand, almost tearing off his penis. He screamed again. She knew she had to move. She lifted the heavy weapon and put one last bullet through his forehead. It slammed him another three feet backward, half under the bed. Valerie ran to the window and looked out. No one was in the alley. She picked up her reticule and crawled out the window, her skirt flapping by the time she got to the ground four feet below. Then she settled her skirts, held the six-gun in a fold of the reticule, and walked straight away from the hotel, angling toward the street. When she was 100 feet removed from the hotel she heard some shouts behind her, but she didn't turn around. She walked on past the house and up to the next street, which was lined with houses. There she

70

took off the sunbonnet and wrapped the six-gun in it and carried it under her arm.

It took Valerie another ten minutes to walk back to her hotel. There she went up to her room, locked the door, pulled out the four spent cartridges and inserted three new ones, letting the hammer down on the empty chamber.

Then she lay down on the bed and tried to cry. She couldn't. Her tears had been spent when Ed died and the day after. She had no remorse for taking another human life. Chug Rollins would be missed by few. She lay there on her back staring at the ceiling.

It was almost a half hour later when a knock sounded on the door. She stared at it but didn't move. The knock came again. She sat up. Who would be coming? The sheriff? No. Spur! She jumped up and ran to the door.

"Who is it?"

"Spur."

She unlocked the door at once and swung it open. He came in and closed the door. She ran into his arms.

"Afternoon, Mrs. Bainbridge."

She held him and wouldn't look up. He put his arms around her, then picked her up and carried her to the bed, where he sat down and draped her across his lap.

"You found one of the men," he said. "I heard something about it. From what everyone said it was either a poor marksman or somebody wanted old Chug to suffer."

She looked up. "He suffered some, but most important, he knew who I was and that he hadn't killed me and that I was the one who evened the score with him.

And he was afraid. After I shot him first in the balls he was scared and furious and crying like a baby."

He held her.

"Was it worth it? Vengeance always has a price. You're paying the piper right now for part of it. There will be more. How strong are you?"

"Strong enough to kill one more. All I have to do is find him. The other one shot Ed. Shot him down with no more concern than swatting a fly. I want him the most. I want to find Mort and make him suffer a long time."

Spur nodded. "I do know how you feel. But in my job I usually don't get the freedom to move quite as swiftly as you have." He bent and kissed her cheek. "Lady, what you need now is a good bottle of wine, a nice supper and a ride in a buggy along the river. The most romantic thing to happen will be the corks popping from the wine bottles."

She stared at him. "I don't want to go."

"Of course you don't, but I say I'm taking you, and since I'm bigger and stronger than you are, I think you'll agree to go peacefully."

A touch of a smile brightened her mouth, then vanished. She nodded.

"But first, I'd say you should change clothes. A lot of folks saw you walking around in that dress and near the hotel. While they won't be looking for a woman, it doesn't do any harm to be careful."

She nodded. He unbuttoned the fasteners down the back and she slipped out of the dress and put on the one she had worn that morning as unconcerned with Spur watching her as if he were her sister. He buttoned up the front of the blue dress for her and then took her downstairs to the general store where he bought her a blue sunbonnet. He had the kitchen prepare a picnic supper for two and asked for two bottles of wine. Then they were off in a rented buggy, out the river road a mile to a grove of trees that was often used for outings. He built a small fire and they ate the sandwiches and then crunched on peanut brittle candy. She ate half a sandwich, but not because she was hungry. The candy was better. By the time Spur opened the wine the sun was down and a bit of a coolness touched the mountain air. She leaned back against him and sighed.

"You're right, the payment does go on for a while. How long?"

"Depends on the person. With Chug, maybe ten seconds. With you, maybe a week, a month. Time is the universal healer. As you let the memory of your husband's death fade into the past, your payments will go down."

"I'm only half done."

"You're still set on killing the other one?"

"Yes, as soon as I can. He's registered at the same hotel. I'll watch outside until I spot him leaving. My guess is that he'll run. Rawhiders won't know who was after them. Probably there's a dozen or two dozen who want to kill them both. If he runs, I'll chase him. First thing in the morning I'll watch."

Spur started picking up the supper. "No. You'll watch tonight. We'll both watch tonight. If he's running he'll go as soon as he sobers up and gets back to his

73

room. There's a chance he is flaked out in some whore house and doesn't even know his partner is dead.''

"Yes,'' she said.

They drove back to town at once. She went to her room, put her hair up so it would fit under a wide-brimmed, low-crowned man's hat she had bought. She put on a small man's shirt and her pants. Then she hid her hair under the hat.

Spur had sat in the chair watching.

"Smudge some dust or dirt on your cheeks, one at least, and take longer steps than usual. You could be a sixteen-year-old boy.''

"Thanks, I guess. Just so it works. I can't chase him in skirts.'' She had strapped on the old Colt. Spur moved it up a little so it didn't ride quite so low.

"You don't want to look like a gunslinger, just a kid who is hanging around town. If he hasn't gone already, and he doesn't move out before about ten tonight, you probably should call it quits for the night. I'll be watching you, case you meet any problems. Just keep to yourself. Sit in a chair or lean against the wall. If you have to say anything, talk low and husky, one or two words.''

"Right,'' she said in a low tone.

"Fine, fine. Now get down there and I'll find you''

She left and Spur was behind her. She locked the door, pushed the key into her pants pocket and walked down the hall.

"A little longer step, don't swagger, but a little more. There, that's it. A boy kind of walk, a little loose jointed. You won't have any trouble.''

He let her go down the stairs alone and out the front

74

door. Then he went through the side door and two blocks down to the Montana Hotel. At the desk he slid the clerk a silver dollar.

"I'm looking for a Dr. Mort Sawtell. Is he registered here?"

The clerk checked his registration book.

"No sir, no Dr. Sawtell. We have a Mort Sawtell, but I think he checked out." The clerk looked again. "Oh, yes, *that* Mr. Sawtell. One of his friends was killed down the hall earlier today. He asked to have a different room and not to give out his number. I'm sure you understand."

"Oh, I was planning on meeting him. Perhaps I could leave a message? Tell him Dr. Jonas Abercrombie will be in town for two more days. He knows my location. That's all the time I have to spend here. Print my name, and get it to him." Spur looked at him sharply. "Young man, I don't like spending a whole dollar and not getting my money's worth. Be sure he gets the message."

The clerk nodded as he wrote. Spur turned and walked across the lobby and up the hallway. As soon as he was out of sight he edged back to the wall and watched the clerk. The message went into the rack of cubbyhole boxes in back of the desk. It was in the top row of boxes, third one from the end. Easy. Spur waited a moment and went back to the clerk, breathing heavily as if he had been running.

"Oh, clerk, that note for Dr. Sawtell. Put on it that I have the required captial with me. We mustn't forget that."

The clerk nodded. Spur looked at him, and beyond

him to the row of boxes. The top row, third from the right end had key 304 hanging from it. Spur spun around and walked out the main entrance.

At first he didn't think she was there. He walked across the street in the shadows and saw a figure sitting in a chair next to the barbershop. He looked like a kid, a youngster not quite ready to do a man's work, but tired of school. He was Valerie.

Spur leaned against the wall beside her.

"Just checked the hotel. Your man is still there, but he moved his room. Good hunting. If nothing turns up here, I'll see you at ten o'clock."

Spur moved down, across the street, and walked into a saloon. He was out three minutes later with a bottle of beer. McCoy found a chair and tilted it back against the side of the bar and watched Valerie. She was doing a good job. He was surprised how natural she looked. In the dark there was no problem with her softly feminine face.

Two hours later she was still there. He went over to her, motioned, and they walked back to the Mountain Lodge Hotel and up to her room. Inside, he took off her hat, fluffed out her hair and kissed her lips softly.

"You've had a tough day. Tonight you sleep alone, you need the rest. If all goes well, I'll see you in the morning in your barbershop chair. He can't stay holed up forever."

Spur went to the door. She sat down on the bed, her eyes holding a fatigued, emotionally drained glaze.

"Spur?"

"Yes."

76

"Thanks. I'll make it. But I'm starting to pay."

"I know. Try not to think about it. Think of only good things, good times, and go right to sleep."

He smiled at her as he closed the door, and he waited for her to lock it. Then he went to his own room, ready for a good night's sleep himself.

CHAPTER SEVEN

Spur looked out his second-floor window, breathed in the cool night air and closed the sash and locked it. He drew the blind and then locked his door, leaving the key in it half turned, and set a straight-backed chair under the knob so the door wouldn't open without making a crashing lot of noise. He checked the loads in his Colt, eased it under his pillow and put his hand on it as he lay down. Hotels like this made him nervous. There were too many ways to get at a person. That night he slept in his clothes and left his boots on. He would be instantly awake and diving for the floor at the least strange or unusual noise.

But there were none, and he woke at 5:30 A.M. as his mental alarm clock told him, had a big breakfast in the hotel dining room, and was first in line at the barbershop when it opened at seven. He had his mustache and muttonchops trimmed and his red hair cut, left full and longer than most men carried it, but the way he liked it, just brushing his collar. He paid his two bits with a newly minted quarter and took a turn in the morning sun in front of the hair trimmer's. He saw Valerie walking down the sidewalk. She was going too slow, and her steps were delicate. But Spur didn't correct her. She sat in a chair on the other side of the door. He saw that she had some trouble keeping all of her hair under the hat, but she had smudged her face. She would pass. Her six-gun was in its usual position.

Spur sat there for half an hour, then got up and passed Valerie.

"Just take it easy and rest yourself," he said softly. "I got to go see about a newspaper."

He continued up the street to the newspaper office. He had seen a black man and Kathleen Smith enter five minutes before. When he got there the door was unlocked and he walked in.

"Well, the land baron is back," Kathleen said.

"True—a junior baron, however. When is your next edition? I'm hoping you'll have room for a small ad."

"We always have room." She held out her hand. "I'm Kathleen Smith," she said. He shook her hand.

"So I've heard. My name is McCoy, Spur McCoy."

She nodded. "Now we can get down to business, Mr. McCoy. What size of ad would you like?"

They worked out the details and the copy, and she said they would have it set in type so he could check a proof at 11:30.

"So soon?"

"If we get the ads set up as we go, then we don't have a big rush on press day."

"Nice little paper you have here. I thought it would

79

be larger, but I know it depends on the amount of advertising the merchants will do. Most towns this size live or die by the kind of newspaper they have. It's interesting traveling around and checking the local papers."

"Oh, who do you travel for?"

"Myself, looking for land. My old father said land was one thing that would always be there. Businesses come and go, buildings rise and fall, but the land is forever."

"Interesting. Why don't you wait a minute and I'll get the printer to look at this and see if there's anything we can't do."

He nodded. She made some more notes on the margin of the four-inch, two-column ad, then went into the back of the shop through the hanging curtain.

He read part of the paper while she was gone. When she came back he thought she had added a little pink rouge to her cheeks but he wasn't sure. Her eyes were bright.

"Mr. McCoy, the ad will be done just after noon. I've got a parcel of property I'd like to show you. No sense knowing the town's business first if I can't turn a profit. Would you object to taking a small buggy ride and looking at it?"

"Not at all, Miss Smith."

"And since it will be getting on toward noon before we get back, would you object if we stopped for a picnic lunch?"

"That sounds delightful, Miss Smith."

"Please, call me Kathleen. I'll have the rig hitched up and brought around. In the meantime I might be able to do a story about you for next week's edition."

"No, I don't think so. I work best when all of the other land speculators don't even know I'm in town. I have been known to change my name two or three times a day just to keep out of the public eye."

"Did you say you were a speculator or a swindler, Mr. McCoy?"

The both laughed. "Well, Kathleen, I always figure the man or woman who can't make a good living by wits alone is just too dumb to be able to enjoy life anyway. Not that I do much that is underhanded or even illegal. But some folks have said that I stretch the truth now and then. But I guess everyone does that."

He watched her, and saw her grin. He was trying for a little bit of sympathy, a comrades-in-arms type of feeling. Honor among thieves. Anyone who would admit to what he did publicly would steal the last crumbs from his starving mother privately.

"I think you and I are going to get along fine, Spur McCoy." She hesitated. "McCoy? Have I heard that name before?"

"Damn, I hope not. I just put it together this week. Hope I didn't pick out the name of some Western gunslinger or something. That would be great, somebody calling me out for a gunfight!"

"Great as in good or bad?" she asked.

"Kathleen, if you had ever seen me use a pistol you wouldn't have to ask." He laughed and they went out to the buggy. She stopped at a restaurant and a short time later came out with a basket. She was smiling as she gave him the reins.

'Just like a picnic in the park," she said.

"You've been to a lot of parks?"

"No, I've read about them."

They talked of the countryside and the weather, and two miles out of town she directed him to pull toward the river side of the road. They went down a narrow trail for a quarter of a mile into a thick stand of aspen. She waved at a sward of untouched green grass, with aspen around the back and edges and the sparkling little river in front.

"Beautiful," he said. She smiled as he helped her down from the one-horse rig and brought the basket and a blanket which he spread out on the grass.

"This is part of the piece of land I wanted to show you," she said. "It's about fifty acres and it has a good price. You want to take a walk around it?"

He shook his head. "No. I'm not that much of a con man. I don't want to buy land out here away from town. But I wouldn't tell you that before we got here. I enjoy going places with a beautiful woman. Let's sit down and talk."

They sat, respectfully separated.

She smiled. "So actually you brought me out here under false pretenses."

She looked at him directly, her smile still there.

"Actually it was *you*, Kathleen, who brought *me* out here. I was just along for the ride." They both grinned. "You're the first girl I've seen in a year who I didn't have to look down on."

"I think that's a compliment."

"It is. Could I ask one favor. Could I kiss you without anyone getting upset?"

"Oh, I think that might be arranged." He slid toward

her and she turned so her breasts touched him as their lips met. The first was a soft one, and he leaned back. Then his arm went around her and his kiss was firmer, more demanding, and she pushed her breasts against his chest. The kiss was longer. His lips left hers but he held her close.

"Let's try that again," she said.

This time as he kissed her they leaned slowly back to the blanket, stretching out, lips tightly together. She rolled toward him until their bodies touched all the way down. Their lips parted.

"Delicious," Spur said. "Are you angry, upset?"

She kissed his lips softly and pulled back. "Do I look angry? I would have been upset if you *hadn't* wanted to kiss me. I'm a very direct person, Spur. I've wanted you to kiss me that way since you first walked into the office."

"We made that wish come true." He kissed her again, and this time she moved so he lay partly on top of her. When their lips parted this time she beamed.

"I think we're getting the hang of it. You see anything else you like?"

He laughed. "I like all of you."

"Pick a spot."

His hand moved over one of her breasts and cupped it, then when she didn't object he rubbed it gently through the fabric of her blouse. The very size of her breasts amazed him and as he rubbed them, he realized they weren't just bulk, they were perfectly formed, firm, and did not sag a bit. He felt the heat coming from them through her clothes. He fumbled with the buttons now as he looked around. She noticed his eyes.

83

"There's no one within miles of here, that's why I picked this spot. I hoped you might get some romantic ideas. If my blouse is getting in your way, why don't you help me take it off?"

He leaned back and looked at her, then bent and pecked a kiss on her mouth.

"Lady, you know where this is leading?"

"Yes, I'm a big girl, and I've wanted to see you all naked and hard ever since yesterday. Now don't talk so damn much."

Her hands began opening the buttons on her blouse and he helped. She wore only one thin petticoat and the usual chemise. With her blouse off he worked his hands under the chemise and caught her breasts. He hadn't realized just how large they were.

"Let's get rid of the rest of these clothes," he said, his voice husky. The blood was pounding in his throat, his neck, and his groin was exploding with the pressure as he lifted her petticoats over her head and she undid the chemise. He felt his penis surge and a stinging sensation shoot through his whole body.

They sat up, and as the chemise came away her breasts surged out in full view. Spur knew he had never seen larger, more perfect breasts. They were symmetrical, placed high on her chest and so firm and solid even their own weight did not let them sag. They had the largest pink areolas he had ever seen, and her nipples were brownish pink, the size of thimbles, filled now with hot blood and a half inch long. His mouth lowered and closed around one and he was amazed at how much he sucked into his mouth and how much tit there was left. He chewed and worked it around for a moment and then realized she was pulling at his clothes.

"Strip, you big fucker!" she said. She grinned at his surprised look. "Do you mind if I talk dirty? It sends me wild. Get your pants off. I want to see your big hairy cock."

He pulled off his shirt, pants and men's drawers and she yelped with anticipation as they came down. When his erection swung out she moaned in absolute delight.

"Oh, yes, sweetness! Beautiful. Stick him in me right now! I can't wait another minute. Right now!" She rolled on her back, half off the blanket, and spread her legs and lifted her knees.

"No love play, no more warmup?" he asked.

"Shit, Spur, I'm so hot right now I'll probably melt that nub of yours off at the roots. Jam it in me and let's see."

Spur knelt beside her, laughing. "You're the most romantic girl I've ever known."

"Hell, Spur, this ain't romance. This ain't even making love. This is just bare-asses fucking! Hard and fast and get it off while you can." Her smile softened. "Now the third and fourth time today will be slower, more gentle."

Spur went between her large but well-formed thighs and marveled again at the size of her. He was more used to girls five feet tall, not nearly six feet tall. Everything was proportionately larger.

"Come on, come on, it won't bite you," she said.

He lowered and drove into her and she gasped in surprise. She knew he was big but hadn't translated that into new, deeper penetration striking long undisturbed places.

Kathleen Smith let out a whoop that could be heard for miles, and then a long, excited scream of pleasure. Spur nearly fell away from her. Then she clamped her arms around his back and he thought he might very well die right there before she let loose. "I must have found the right spot," he said.

She moaned and looked up. "Quit talking, man, and fuck!"

He laughed and drove at her, and he knew it when she climaxed. She exploded with another scream and pushed his hips three feet in the air with hers, then dropped down, and now they were totally sprawled on the grass.

Her large hips pounded up at him now on every stroke. She wailed and screamed, her arms held him tightly and her long legs wrapped around his torso, her ankles locking around each other. She brought them higher still and at last he moved his arms and she put her legs on his shoulders, lying almost bent double below him.

Spur slammed ahead now at the new angle and in ten pounding, driving strokes he dissolved. The whole world melted into a giant pool of ice-cold water and he plunged into it, diving deep to the very center of the frozen universe through a black-hole tunnel, and came out in a different universe entirely, where up was down and black was white.

He exploded with a series of hip thrusts that blasted his mind into outer space and he let her legs down, then fell on her ample body, panting and knowing that he would die happy now.

Five minutes later he came away from Kathleen and

lay beside her on the cool grass.

"Christ, you didn't tell me you were a succubus in disguise," Spur said.

"What is that? It sounds dirty."

"A succubus is a demon in female form who seduces men in their sleep. The idea goes back to 1661. You're a lot older than you look."

She laughed. "Sounds like a good job. Suppose there's much demand for that sort of thing?"

"It all depends on your connections with the Devil, and he's sometimes hard to pin down."

"Then I'll just hang around and work for you. God, but that was great. It's been a long time since I been done that good. I mean, you were fantastic!" She grinned. "And I ain't no blushing virgin crooning over my first cock."

"You inspired me." He reached over and fondled her breasts. At once she sat up so they would show at their best. "I have never seen anything so beautiful," Spur said.

"Men just love tits," Kathleen said.

"True, but these are special. Not just bulk and fat and mass, but finely proportioned for you, firm and strong and holding up. Just fantastic."

"You're starting to sound like we have time for a couple more," she said.

"Not after the way you wore me out that time. I'll be a week trying to recuperate."

"Don't shit me, Spur."

"True. I was here to relax and rest, but on the trail I met this little nymphomaniac who wouldn't let me get to sleep nights until we had three go-rounds. That wears a man out in a rush. And besides, I made a damn date to see my banker at two this afternoon.''

''Shit!''

''Sorry, but it isn't the end of the world. Maybe I can invite you up to my hotel room one of these nights where we could use a bed and have some champagne like real people.''

''Is that a proposition?''

''You just name the date, lovely lady.'' He stroked her breasts and saw she was getting excited again.

''Tonight, ten o'clock, your hotel room.''

''Tonight? Hey give me twenty-four hours to recuperate. How about tomorrow night? I may be changing hotels to something better. I'll see you tomorrow in the afternoon to look at that ad and firm up the time.''

She reached over and kissed him. ''That's a bargain.'' She looked at the water. ''Since we're in our swimming suits, do you want to splash in the water?''

''Looks cold. That's snow melt, isn't it?''

''Probably. Might be cold enough to freeze my tits off, but let's try it.'' She stood and ran to the water, her large breasts swinging from side to side.

He followed her. He hadn't been skinny-dipping since he was ten. She waded into the shallow stream and when the water came to her knees she turned around and walked right back out.

''God, it's freezing cold.'' She looked down quickly at her breasts. ''Good, both of them are still there.''

They dressed, then ate the picnic lunch and threw stones in the water. She was half angry with him.

''What a waste, throwing rocks in the river when we could be making love in the grass.''

"Patience. The forbidden—in this case the *delayed* fruits—are always sweeter." She snorted and he didn't know if she believed him or not.

It was almost one o'clock when Spur drove the buggy up to the Wallace Livery Stable. He turned the rig in after he let Kathleen Smith off a half block from her newspaper office.

As he got out of the buggy he saw Deputy Sheriff Cyrus Mercer talking with a stablehand. Cyrus waved at Spur and ambled over with a gait any sailor would be proud of.

"Afternoon, Mr. McCoy."

"Afternoon, Deputy Mercer. Think the rain will hurt the rhubarb?"

"Fact is, McCoy, that's just what I wanted to talk to you about. You got a minute?"

"Likely."

Mercer pointed up the street and they walked that way.

"I think I got you in trouble with the sheriff, son. I told him you were in town and he said he thought he recognized your name. He did some thinking and now he's rawhiding me to find you. He's got a long hair up his ass about something, and I don't like it one bit. People have a history of disappearing around this town, especially when Sheriff Amos Hanshoe don't like them."

CHAPTER EIGHT

Spur McCoy stared at the deputy. "Sheriff Hanshoe say what was bothering him?"

"Not so you could notice. He said to bring you in unarmed and under my gun if I had to. He's in a snit about something."

"And in this mood he could be dangerous?"

"Been known to happen."

"He charging me with that shooting yesterday?"

"Nope, he's not much concerned about that one. It's something else, something about your name, I think. He had me point you out yesterday and he paced around his office half the afternoon. Don't know what the hell's bothering him."

They walked the block to the sheriff's office and jail and Spur went in the door first.

"Spur McCoy?" a booming voice demanded.

Spur looked to the left and saw a man with a six-gun in hand. It looked as if he had been practicing a fast draw. Sheriff Hanshoe stood barely five feet tall. He had on a leather vest over a plaid shirt and string tie. Over his pants he wore leather chaps with fancy fringes and beads on them. He looked like a dime novel cowboy. His face was fleshy, with a large nose that must have been broken and beaten dozens of times and never quite returned to its normal size, puffy cheeks, slitted beady black eyes and a half bald head with fringes of brown hair on both sides. His ears were the largest Spur had ever seen.

"That's right, I'm McCoy."

"This is him, Sheriff," Mercer said. "He came in on his own, no trouble."

"Good," the sheriff said. "Out, Mercer." Sheriff Hanshoe put the cut-down Colt in his holster and walked with a limp to the big desk and sat behind it on a higher than normal chair.

"I should throw you in jail and lose the key, McCoy. I know who you are now. The name started it and then I remembered once I was in St. Louis when all hell cut loose and you was behind most of it. I wondered at the time how you could go around shooting up so many people and then walk away. I finally found out."

"Sheriff, I'm busy. I've got a lot of things to do. Am I under arrest? If so, arrest me. If not, I'm walking out that door in about twenty seconds."

The sheriff stood and tried his fast draw. The front sights tangled in the leather, the gun dropped from his hand and fired as it hit the wooden floor.

The door burst open to the jail and two deputies rushed in with drawn guns.

The sheriff roared at them. "Get out of here!" The

deputies backed out the door and closed it.

Hanshoe had picked up his weapon by then and pushed it back in his leather.

"What I found out about you, McCoy, is that you are a federal man. A goddamned government lawman of some kind. I dunno what—a U.S. Marshal, a special deputy, something. Now, I had government lawmen through here before. They always stop in, say hello, tell me what the problem is and together we take care of it. Now, you didn't do that, boy."

"Sheriff, I don't owe you a damn thing. If I am a federal lawman of some kind, I have jurisdiction in every state and territory in these United States. And that includes La Plata County. Now, I don't have any idea what you got going here, Sheriff, and I don't want to know because then I might figure I had to take care of that too. I've got an assignment in this county and I'm going to handle it. I'll do it with or without your help or your hindrance. As you say, most U.S. lawmen cooperate with the local authorities, but not always. There could have been half a dozen U.S. Marshals in town and you never knew about it. Now, it's your turn. Are you arresting me for something, or are you going to apologize for disturbing a citizen about his normal business?"

Hanshoe paced around the room, his hands behind his back, the big gun slapping his thigh. He stopped from time to time and stared at Spur.

"What the hell you threatening me for, McCoy? I'm just trying to do my job. Sure I get jealous when you federal lawmen come sweeping into town. I try to help. Little thanks I get."

He paced again.

"Take you. Big shot from St. Louis. Here after one of our citizens. How does it look in the paper when you make the arrest? Hell, I got to get elected in this town, you don't. You can at least confer with me. I might know something about the case you're working on."

"Sheriff, this is a highly delicate matter. When I came here I didn't even know who the suspects were. Now at least I have a general direction. When it's time to arrest the perpetrators and bring them to justice, I'll be sure to bring you in on all the glory. You can even lead the charge if we have to battle them with pistols at point blank range."

"Oh, well, I never. . . . That is, as sheriff *I* can't be put in a dangerous position. That's why I have deputies. They take all the chances. But I'll certainly be ready to help you jail the suspects and to talk to the newspaper for you."

"I'm sure you will, Sheriff. Now, if there's nothing else, I do have some things to do."

"Yes, yes. Go ahead. I'm just small potatoes out here in the wilds of Colorado Territory. Now if we was a state . . ."

"It wouldn't be any different," Spur said. "If I need you on this case, I'll give a yell. And until I do I'd rather you just forget about me. I'd just as soon everyone in town didn't know I was here."

"Who are the guys you're after?" Hanshoe asked.

"When I arrest them, you'll know," Spur said. He turned and left the room. On the boardwalk outside, Deputy Cyrus Mercer fell in step beside Spur.

"Sorry about old Hanshoe. He's elected for four years, this is his second. He'll never get elected for another term. Hell, I'll run against him if I have to. You want any help, anybody to back you, just give a call."

Spur nodded and Cyrus turned into the next saloon. The tall Secret Service agent continued up the street to the barbershop and leaned against the wall. A youth not much over sixteen sat in the chair.

"Anything happening?" Spur asked.

"Nothing. I could cry."

"Hey, men don't cry, not out here in the wild West. I'll meet you in your room in about five minutes. Time you took a break. You have any noontime food?"

"No."

"I'll meet you in the dining room. No, then you'd have to change. I'll get some food and bring it up to your room."

A half hour later she was finishing a huge chicken, ham and tomato sandwich, a big glass of milk and two cinnamon rolls.

"Oh, I heard all about you," she told him. "Just before you came, two men walked by talking about you and they said you was a federal marshal in town to capture someone. They said they weren't even sure who you were, but one man said he'd seen you."

"Damn. That sheriff has a big mouth. He was supposed to keep it shut. Now it's going to be harder than before to nail down these people I'm hunting."

"I saw you in the buggy with that tall woman," Valerie said. "Do you like her? I mean, she's tall and has big . . . . She's more your size."

"Sure, I like her. When I'm on a case I like everyone. You never can tell who might give you the lead to solve a case. I even like you."

She stuck her tongue out at him. Spur laughed and kissed her cheek.

"If you weren't obviously a boy, I'd kiss you properly."

"Maybe you could tonight," she said softly. "I mean if you're not going to be impaled on those big breasts that woman has." Valerie looked up, grinning. "I feel just so wicked saying that." She sobered. "You know you said I'd have to pay. I guess I'm still paying. I didn't get a lot of sleep last night."

"Don't think about it. You did what you thought was right. It will fade. Believe me, I know. It will become less and less important. And you'll go back to Denver or St. Louis and meet an exciting young man and get married again." He bent and kissed her soft lips and she pushed forward just a little and clung to the kiss for a few seconds. Her eyes turned up to him.

"Spur McCoy, I should marry you. You seem to know all the right things to say. You can find me all dead and worn out and in the blues, and make me smile and grin and feel just ever so much better. You're so much different from most of the men I've known. They have to be rough and tough all the time. They have to prove to me they are stronger and can make me have sex with them. Or they ignore me and don't think I can add two and two."

"But I'm as fickle as an old tom cat, remember that," Spur said. "Didn't I dump you as soon as we got to town and I had a good bath?"

She grinned. "I'm going to look for Mort until eleven tonight. I'll take my watch. If I don't find him I'll start asking around at the saloons and the bawdy houses."

"You stay away from them."

"We'll see. I better get back to my post. I've changed places two or three times. I wonder if he's already left town?"

"I think he's still here," Spur said. "Even if he isn't, you've taken care of two of the three of them."

She nodded. "I've thought about that." She reached up and kissed his lips quickly, then went to the door. She turned and watched him. "Hey, will I see you here tonight?"

"I've got to make some late night calls on some businesses after the owners go home. I'll see how it goes. I can't watch you tonight out there, so be careful. If all else fails, pull off your hat and flare out your hair. That will stop anybody from hurting you."

When Valerie left for her lookout spot again, Spur returned to his own room and arranged for hot bathwater in the first floor bath. He soaked and scrubbed and then put on a new white shirt with a row of shell buttons up the front. His string tie topped his attire and was followed by a pair of black broadcloth trousers. He put on a soft, gray doeskin vest and his gray low-crowned Stetson and was ready to go do some banking.

It was called the Colorado State Bank, and as far as Spur could tell it was doing a good business. He asked two clerks and at last discovered the president of the establishment, one Isaac Quigley. He was a tall, thin man in a black suit and wide tie, with a monocle perched in his right eye.

Spur sat down beside the golden oak desk and tried a smile on Mr. Quigley. He got a frown back.

"Yes, now, I was told you had a matter of some

urgency, sir."

"I do, Mr. Quigley. It is a bit embarrassing. I came from Denver not long ago and while there I picked up considerable cash in the form of U.S. bank notes, and later I heard that there was a large problem there with spurious notes. Counterfeit. I was wondering could you check over my currency and tell me if any I have are . . . bad bills?"

"What? Well, certainly. Duty and all that sort of thing. We can't have counterfeit bills floating around, can we? Now what denomination were they?"

"Twenties."

"Dear me. That would be expensive. Let's see them."

Spur took out a new wallet and produced four almost new twenty-dollar bills. They were the 1862 series of United States Notes, also known as Legal Tender Notes because of the stipulation on the back in a circle between the denomination numbers. He put the four bills on the desk, and the banker looked at them closely, then picked them up and felt the paper. He at once put one of the bills to one side, then another. At last he laid the third note on the stack and waved the fourth.

"This one is bad. You can *feel* it, a difference in the paper. The workmanship is excellent. I'm afraid I'll have to confiscate this note and return it to the federal treasury."

"That's fine. Just replace it with a legitimate bill, please."

"Oh, that's impossible."

"Then you don't get the other one." Spur snatched the bill from the man's hand and scooped up the other bills. "Sir, I'm no stranger to banking. You are authorized only to impound counterfeits that come through your bank. This bill has not left my possession, is not on deposit in your bank, and you have no rights to the bill. I'm not going to lose twenty dollars just to satisfy your sense of duty."

"Then why did you come here today?" the banker asked.

"I told you, to identify any bad money I might have. I don't remember that I offered to deposit any funds with you."

The banker nodded. "Very well, that matter is closed. Now, I wish to be ultimately certain that those bills you showed me did not come from Durango. Can you swear positively that you brought that particular bill, the bad one, with you from Denver?"

Spur nodded. "Oh, yes. Definitely. I had five bills and I folded them and placed them in an envelope and put it in the very bottom of my carpetbag so I couldn't lose them. Yes, definitely. Not a chance that I picked up the counterfeit here in Durango."

The sweating banker nodded again and led Spur to the side door.

"I would appreciate it if you kept this quiet. Any mention of counterfeit bills could cause a near panic here. We take the bank notes at face value, as you know, and any lowering of their accepted value . . . I'm sure you understand the problem."

Spur said he was aware of the situation, and he would keep silent about the bad paper bills.

He smiled as he stepped into the street. An hour later he was in a saloon nursing a warming beer when he heard the first rumor.

The hardware store man came in. He was furious. Said the bank had told him that all twenty dollar bills would have to be inspected before deposit. There was a possibility of counterfeit bills circulating.

Spur knew how the rumor and the whole idea of the worth of the paper money would spread. It wouldn't do any real damage, but it would give the counterfeiters plenty of internal problems. Someone was bound to accuse another one of spending some of the phony money here in Durango. Spur would just as soon have the tight little organization blow itself to bits from the inside.

He had supper with Valerie. She had given up her disguise, taken a bath and put on her best dress. She was bright and gay and happy. Spur was afraid she was becoming serious about him. He left her right after supper. His schedule called for him to go to his room and sleep until midnight. Then he would go visit the newspaper and see if he could find any green ink and special U.S. bank note printing papers.

CHAPTER NINE

Spur tossed and turned on the bed. He had taken off his boots and shirt at seven and blown out the kerosene light. But he couldn't sleep. Something bothered him. He thought back over the day's events, and slowly it filtered through.

Danger.

He was a target. He could feel it. Something had tipped off the counterfeiters. It couldn't have been the romp with Kathleen. The government-man-in-town talk could have done it. He got up, lit the lamp and used a spare blanket and his carpetbag to make a passable-looking dummy under the sheets in his bed. Then he put on his shirt and boots, turned down the lamp, and raised his second floor window. No sense making it hard for them if they were coming. He took the last blanket and laid it along the window wall and tried to go to sleep.

Anyone on a ladder would touch the outer wall and

he would be alerted at once. They would fire into the dummy on the bed and Spur would blast them out of the window with his .44. He turned now with his head toward the window, only six feet from it. He was in the perfect spot. In spite of his best efforts to stay awake, Spur dozed off.

He came awake just after one o'clock when twin blasts from a shotgun roared into his room, ripping apart the bedding and his carpetbag. He shook his head to stop the ringing of the blasts and crawled to the window. All he saw was a man dropping off the end of a rope and jumping on a horse. He was gone before Spur could get off a shot. Spur was still shaking his head when someone from the hall banged on his door. Spur didn't move.

Yes, perfect. He was dead. The gunman had riddled the bed. He hadn't stayed around to see the blood; he'd fired and then dropped down the rope to his horse. Off the roof, down a rope, fire two barrels at once and drop down to the ground.

Perfect. And the unknown assailant had killed Spur McCoy, land buyer. Spur went quietly to the door and removed the chair, then straightened the key. He could hear voices outside, some angry at being awakened, some curious.

At last he heard a stern voice. It was the hotel night manager.

"All right, everyone back. The deputy and me are the only ones getting to look inside the room, so the rest of you go back to bed. You'll find out all about it tomorrow."

A key pushed into the lock. Spur's key fell out on the

floor. The lock opened and Spur edged behind the opening door.

"Git!" a heavy voice said. Spur could hear feet walking down the hall. The door came open and a lamp came in first, followed by a bare arm, and then the deputy jumped in, his six-gun out and cocked. The light filled the room.

"Okay, nobody here," Deputy Mercer said.

"You sure, Cyrus?" the manager asked.

Spur closed the door and spoke rapidly.

"Cyrus, don't shoot, it's McCoy."

The six-gun came around fast and Spur could see pressure on the trigger, then the light from the lamp washed over Spur and Cyrus lowered the Colt.

"Jesus, what happened in here?"

"Somebody killed me tonight," Spur said.

Cyrus grinned. "Looks like they sure as hell did."

The night manager, a short man with robust arms and a full beard, shook his head.

"But you're McCoy, and this is your room. You sure as hell ain't dead."

"But they think I am, whoever tried to kill me. Two barrels of double-ought buck at fifteen feet is gonna kill anybody—right, Cyrus?"

"You bet. Bill, you just say what I tell you to. This is police business. Sheriff's office. We come in here and we found McCoy here shot up so bad nobody could recognize him, and we took him over to the undertaker. Body is so blasted up don't nobody want to look at it, and we'll bury him all proper tomorrow afternoon."

"You mean . . . and the guy that shot . . . Oh, I

102

see. Yeah."

"And you'll tell it exactly the way we say?"

"Sure. Damn, this is fun."

"A body, Cyrus. You got a body?" Spur asked.

"Had a drifter stabbed tonight. Blood all over an alley. We can use him. Yancy the undertaker will go along with it for twenty dollars."

Spur took a twenty from his wallet and gave it to Cyrus, then offered one to the night manager.

"No sir, can't bribe me. I'll do it just to help Cyrus nail the killer. I'm a good citizen."

"Fine. Get out in the hall and make sure all of the people there have gone to bed. Then get about a quart of chicken blood and whatever else you can find and smear it around the bed and the walls. I've got to salvage what I can of my clothes and that carpetbag."

A half hour later it was done. Spur had shifted his belongings into Valerie's room. She listened wide-eyed as he told her what had happened. Then he went back to his room and down the rope to the ground. He had on a black shirt now, the same as his pants, and ran quickly to the alley behind the newspaper office. The only open window he could find was on the second floor. He went up a big aspen tree near the back of the two-story building and with a short piece of rope climbed from the roof to an open window and went through. He was on the balcony of a small second floor stacked with records and boxes. Spur made a careful survey of the whole building. One night light burned in back, a safety lamp made all of metal except for the small chimney, with a fire catcher around it. There was no one in the plant, front or back.

Spur began a systematic search of the rear of the building. He found printing papers of fifty different hues, shapes and colors, but none of them were of the consistency or fibrous construction that was the same as the U.S. bank notes. He went over and under the small job presses and the big flatbed. Nothing.

Spur looked under the trash box, tested the boards on the floor for a secret trap door, went through each box in the upstairs storage—burning his fingers twice when his fingers told him he had found something worth risking the use of a stinker match. Again, no bank-note type paper, no engravings, no boxes of already printed bills. He was sure he would find something. He went to the front office and searched the storage drawers under the countertop, then went through the two desks in the office.

Not a scrap of evidence to show that the three were or had been printing counterfeit twenty-dollar bills.

He was about to give up in frustration when he walked to the curtain separating the front and back parts of the plant. He heard someone unlocking the side door. The person, a man, stumbled inside and closed the door, but couldn't get it locked. Spur waited. The form came toward him, then turned to one side and fell on a cot that had been pushed against the wall. The man carried a double-barreled shotgun. He fell on the bed and passed out almost at once. Spur walked quietly past the man, pausing to look at his face. Full beard, unkempt like his hair. Dirty clothes. A big man, about six feet. Spur would never forget that face. He walked on to the side door, which was still unlocked, pushed through and closed it, then walked slowly to the back door of the hotel. He was baffled. He was sure the three of them were printing the money here in Durango. Why else come here and go to the trouble of establishing this kind of respectable camouflage? They had to be printing money. But where?

Spur pulled his hat down over his eyes and kept to the dark, back streets as he worked to the Mountain Lodge Hotel, then slipped in the back door and up the side stairs without anyone seeing him. He unlocked Valerie's door at 202 and stepped inside.

When he lay down on the bed beside her, she reached out in her sleep, found his shoulder and kept her hand there. In the moonlight through the window he saw her smiling. Good, she needed some pleasant thoughts.

Suddenly Valerie sat up in bed.

"No! No! Don't kill him! Don't kill my husband!" She ended the outburst with a long wailing cry and then slumped back on the bed, lying down slowly. At last the tension left her face and she slept again, but not so peacefully. Her arms were clasped protectively across her breasts.

It was almost seven before he stirred. Spur came awake instantly when he sensed her moving. She sat up and smiled at him.

"Now's the time I wished that I slept naked. I didn't hear you come back last night." She paused. "Do you want me to take off my nightgown?"

He leaned over and kissed her softly. "I wouldn't be any good for you right now. I need some more sleep. Remember, I'm dead, so I'll be doing most of my work at night."

"Then I better get dressed."

"Can I watch?" he asked with a sparkle in his eye.

She smiled and nodded. "Unless it will get you too excited and interfere with your sleep." Suddenly her face clouded. "Oh, no, I forgot. My boobs aren't nearly as big as your tall lady friend's. You might not even see mine."

He grabbed her and kissed her and rubbed one perky breast through her soft white nightgown. When his lips came off hers, she had to gasp in a big breath.

"Valerie Bainbridge, I don't ever want to hear you talking bad about yourself again. You are a beautiful girl, and I'd lots rather make love to you than anybody in this town. But right now I'm exhausted and need some more sleep. You hear me, pretty lady?"

The smile that broke across her face was worth a month's pay to Spur. She gently kissed his cheek, and blinked back tears of surprise and joy.

"Yes sir!" she said. She bounced away from him and pulled off the cotton nightgown, then posed naked, seductively, for him, her bouncing breasts in profile; he could see just a brief swatch of her pubic hair.

He growled at her and she jumped away to the dresser and took out some clothes. She dressed slowly as he watched.

"I'll never get tired watching a beautiful woman dress. It's like a classical ballet. You ever see a ballet?" She shook her head. "A lot of the movements are similar." He yawned and turned over.

"You want some breakfast?" she asked softly.

"I'll have dinner instead. Wake me about twelve if I'm not up." She kissed his cheek and tiptoed out to the

106

hall, locked the door and went down to the dining room.

Spur got up just before twelve and saw Valerie reading a book by the window. Spur nodded and looked through his bullet-riddled carpetbag. He found what he wanted, an old eye patch he wore now and then, a tattered, long, black foul-weather coat and a slouch hat with no blocking left in it, with sides that drooped and worked well in the rain. It would also help hide his face. It should be enough of a disguise. Nobody would be looking for him since he was dead. The only problem might be the sheriff. If he demanded to see the body, it could be trouble. Spur hoped that Cyrus would handle that, but he didn't want to get Cyrus in trouble.

Valerie went to the kitchen and brought up his dinner, a big roast beef sandwich and a bowl of vegetable soup. He thanked her with a kiss and a pat on her round, soft bottom.

"Thank you," she said. Her good smile was back. "I gave up on watching for Mort. I went down by the saloon where he usually spends his time and asked around. Nobody there had seen him for a whole day. They figured when his partner got killed he ran out fast. I'll keep watching for him, but not the way I was."

He finished the sandwich, settled the six-gun on his hip and made sure his cartridge belt was full with the twenty rounds he carried in the small leather loops. Then he picked her up, kissed her mouth, and put her down.

"I'm going to be a housebreaker this afternoon. My big hope is that nobody is home."

"Part of the job?"

"Right."

"Then I hope nobody *is* home." She sighed and blinked back tears. "I worry about you, Spur McCoy. I know, I know. I have no claim and no right, but a girl sometimes can't control her dumb old heart, it just grabs onto what it wants to."

"I know, it's happened to me. Let's just see how things work out." He kissed her cheek and stepped out the door into the hallway after making sure no one was watching.

Spur went down the back stairs and the desk clerk yelled at him to clear out and stay out. Good. He decided he must look disreputable enough. Spur went around Main Street as he meandered along toward Kathleen Smith's house. She had pointed it out on the drive the day before and invited him to stop by any time. She probably meant when she was home. Spur figured the place would be empty now, with her and the printer at the office. He didn't know what the shotgun man did during the day. Spur guessed it had been the third member of the gang who came off the hotel roof and blasted the dummy in the bed, but he couldn't be sure.

The Secret Service agent turned into the alley in back of the house he wanted. There were only three houses on the long street, and none of them were large. This one was of wooden siding and shingles, and he guessed it had about five rooms. At the rear of the place he wandered up to the back door and tried it. Locked. A key ring from his pocket produced the skeleton key type that flipped open the lock, and he edged the door open and stepped into the kitchen.

He paused, every one of his senses alert, eyes darting around, ears straining for the least noise from the house. He had his six-gun out now and had cocked it outside. Quietly he moved to the doorway that led into the rest of the house. A sitting and dining room to the front, two bedrooms to the side, and no upstairs. He checked the big room, then went to the closet doorway and pushed it open. One hinge squeaked. It was a woman's bedroom, and no one was there. The bed wasn't made.

Silently he stepped to the next bedroom, and saw with a start that it must be a man's room. The bed had been made, and men's clothing was scattered around the room. A shotgun and a rifle lay on the bed, and a box of shells, double-ought buck, lay beside them.

He stepped into the room, made certain no one was in the small closet or under the bed. Then he quietly, efficiently went through everything in the room. There were clothes in only the top drawer of the dresser. A saddle in one corner and a coiled rope. He found one more weapon, a new Remington .44 Army revolver and a box of shells. Not much else, little personal gear. He moved to the woman's bedroom and went through her things. She had several times as many clothes and other items as the man. But nowhere did he find anything that would implicate her in the illegal printing trade.

Spur frowned and moved to the living room. Could he have been wrong? It all fit so neatly. He started in a secretary, a tall cabinet with shelves covered by doors with windows in them, shelves at the middle and a fold-out section to make a desk. Drawers in the bottom were for storage. He opened the writing table and went to work. In the fourth cubicle in the front he found a piece of paper that made his heartbeat surge. It was a pen-and-ink drawing to size of the front of a twenty-dollar U.S. note. The seal was there, the bill number—79202—the seal done in red ink and the portrait of some government official on the left side. It was a working model, with exacting detail of every part of the bank note. From this she would make the plate, the engraving to be used in the actual printing. He folded the drawing and put it inside his shirt pocket and kept looking.

A key rattling in the front door brought him out of the room and charging for the back door. Noise didn't matter now. He slammed through the back door and heard someone running after him. Spur ran hard, had out his six-gun to help scare off the chaser if possible.

He looked back, saw a man with a shotgun that he was pulling to his shoulder. Spur was no more than thirty feet away. Just as the man was ready to fire, Spur snapped a shot to the rear.

At the same instant he fired, Spur did a running dive to his right. As he did the shotgun roared with both barrels, and he felt the lead slugs whispering over him. One caught the side of his arm, but by that time he had completed the roll, was on his feet and darting around the next house. Now he had some protection and he sprinted over the empty lot toward the third house. His pursuer had mistakenly guessed that he could stop Spur with both barrels. Now he would have to stop and reload, unless he had a six-gun. The long coat got in the way as Spur surged forward, running hard to get past the next house and then around the corner into Main Street. He heard the shotgun fire again from behind him, but now he was fifty yards away and there was almost no chance of a hit. But Spur did another dive, this time to the left, and came up running, rounded the corner and panted as he walked into a saloon, went straight through and out the back door into the alley, then between two houses and onto the street. He pulled off the long black coat and dumped it into a burn barrel in the alley, took off the old hat, folded it and carried it in his hand as he walked toward the corner. He would curve back to the hotel. By now he was sure he had lost the man. The impression stuck—a big man with a scraggly beard and black hair. Spur had the impression it was the same one he had seen falling down drunk in the newspaper printing plant the night before.

Only then did he think to look at his arm. The bullet had penetrated the long coat and burned a mark across his arm and punched two holes in his shirt. At least it wasn't bleeding. He would get some carbolic to put on it.

Spur put his hat on again and pulled it down. He didn't want anyone who might recognize him to see him. It was much better being dead this way.

CHAPTER TEN

Inside Valerie's room again safely, Spur discarded the eye patch and the slouch hat. He put on a pair of black-rimmed spectacles and stared in the mirror.

"You look like a professor," Valerie said.

"Good." He reached in his wallet and found a five-dollar bill which he gave to the girl. "Go down to the hotel manager and tell him you want to buy some of his lost-and-found clothing. Take a look at it and bring up two pair of pants, an old coat, a couple of hats and a sweater or two. The five dollars can go to the orphans' fund, or to the manager."

"You need some new disguises, right?" she asked. He nodded and she hurried out the door.

A half hour later Spur was outfitted again. His hat was battered and trail weary, a black high-crown with a Texas star on one side and both brims rolled up half-way. The glasses helped and he now had a kerchief around his neck over an old wool shirt and a lightweight jacket of an off-brown color. His pants were brown too, but did not match the jacket. The pants were short and exposed three inches of his boots. Spur strapped on his gunbelt and the trusty .44 and checked in the mirror. No one would guess he was the same black-coated stranger who had been shot at a few minutes ago.

An hour later Spur had toured all but one of the saloons and still hadn't spotted the unkempt watchman from the newspaper office. The man's face kept returning to him but he couldn't match it with a wanted poster. He ordered a beer at the counter and sipped it. This was his fourth beer but he hadn't finished any of them. He picked up the brew and wandered, watching the two poker games in session, unobtrusively checking each man in the place, but there was no sign of his shotgunner. Spur was back at the bar, working on the beer again, when the batwings swung and the man Spur had been looking for came in and went straight to the bar. He still carried his shotgun. The bartender knew him and lifted the scatter gun over the railing for safekeeping. The man downed a straight shot of whiskey in one gulp and put the glass down for another. Spur had a good chance now to watch the man in the six-foot-long mirror in back of the bar.

Yes, he had seen him before—he *was* wanted. But for what, Spur couldn't remember.

Spur turned away and listened, trying to hear what was being said farther down the bar. He caught a little of the exchange.

"Do any good?"

"Hell no. Ran like a rabbit . . ."

". . . Next time."

113

". . . But who the hell was he?"

"Do them marshals come in teams?"

"Damned if I know."

Spur drained his beer and headed for the door. Nothing more he could do here. He'd watch from outside. A sharp command stopped him.

"Hold it! You with the red beard. What the hell you doing?"

Spur turned slowly, his hand quivering an inch from his gun butt. He stared at the shotgunner.

"Yeah, I'm talking to you, Red. You didn't even say goodnight to my buddy the bartender."

It was a roust, to try to get him angry, Spur knew. The shotgunner suspected him, and his damn red beard might have done it. He could play that game too.

"Suh, I am about to blow your white-trash mouth halfway back to Tennessee. I don't cotton to be spoken to in that fashion, suh. And I demand your immediate apology, or you had just better be slapping leather and pulling a trigger!" Spur had layered on the Southern accent with a sudden fury, and the shotgunner blinked. He brought both his hands to the bar, slowly and well away from the hogsleg on his hip.

"Hold on there, Colonel. I was just joshing you a little. Barkeep bet me five dollars you was from Texas, and I said Louisiana. So we both lose. No harm meant, none 'tall."

Spur relaxed a little, but his hand still stayed near the pistol butt.

"Right, suh, you both lose," Spur said in the same dripping accent. "Be sure you don't lose next time on the smoking end of my .44. Goodnight to you-all, suh.

A good night to everyone." Spur walked on out of the saloon, presenting his broad back to the shotgunner who only stood and gawked at him.

Outside Spur vanished into the pool of blackness along the boardwalk between the islands of light from the four saloons. He watched and waited. As he did he took off the tall Texas hat and threw it down the alley, then waited again. He didn't think it would be long for the shotgunner. Spur had picked the direction away from the newspaper office. He figured the bushwhacker would come out after another drink or two and go to the printing plant.

He was right. A half hour later the man came out, the shotgun over his shoulder, and walked with steps just a bit unsteady toward the newspaper. Spur followed him without making a sound. Just as the man opened the side door of the office, Spur put three shots from his .44 into the wood beside him, and the man scrambled inside and slammed the door.

The small attack would give the counterfeiters something to think about—and, he hoped, to talk about. There was still a light in the front of the building, and it snuffed out quickly.

Good, now they would have more to talk about. He turned and went along the alley until he came to the Mountain Lodge Hotel. He had to wait a few minutes until the hallway and the back steps cleared, then hurried up to Valerie's room.

When Pat O'Reilly jumped inside the back door and slammed it, he was both surprised and momentarily afraid. Who in hell would be shooting at him—in the

115

dark—and miss? There were people in town who didn't like him. Pat was not the kind of man to ease through life and not make a few enemies. But they wouldn't gun him down in ambush.

The damn colonel—that honey-dripping, Southern-talking, magnolia-blossom fake colonel! He must have been burned and tried to take a potshot at him. Would the man miss three times? O'Reilly wondered. He heard someone swear and then the light came back on in the front office.

"Pat, that you?" Kathleen's voice asked.

"Either me or some damn big rat back here learned to talk," Pat said. He went past the night lantern and toward the front.

"Time we had a little conference," Kathleen said from the parted curtain at the doorway. "You have a few spare minutes?"

"Hell, yes. Where's the bottle?"

"We don't have one this time," Henry said. "We want some straight answers."

The blind was drawn on the front door and the drapes pulled on the windows facing the street. The three of them sat around the big desk and Kathleen started it.

"Pat, did you hear about the scare that hit town yesterday afternoon and today?"

"The counterfeit thing?" Pat asked. "Nothing to it. Bank said they had not actually taken a single counterfeit bill." Pat looked at the others.

"That's what the banker *says,* Pat. The truth could be much different. Quigley doesn't want to admit there are any fake bills around, because that could cause a run on his bank and ruin him."

"So? So what the hell's that got to do with us?"

"Plenty," Henry said. "I think there are counterfeits in circulation in town. Maybe a lot of them, I don't know. And if they are, our whole operation here is in bad trouble. The first thing the government will do is send one or two or three of its Secret Service men out here like they did to Denver. Remember Denver, Pat? We almost bought a seat in a federal prison there, didn't we?"

"Hey, now, no chance, you two. I told you I learned my lesson. No! I haven't touched any of those just-printed bills. So help me. Why do I need them when I got a thousand dollars worth of real twenties in my kit?"

"A few more wouldn't hurt," Kathleen said. "You could spend the fake ones and save the real ones for later. It's hard to trust you, Pat, after Denver."

"Shit, I'd be crazy to do that. Are any of them missing? You know how many you print, black man. You missing any? Go and count them, goddammit! Don't you ever come accusing me of stealing when you don't know what the fuck you're saying. I don't take that kind of shit off no black sonofabitch!"

O'Reilly had drawn his Tranter six-gun, an 1863 model .44-caliber rimfire, and waved it at Henry.

Kathleen walked in front of him and put her hands on the weapon.

"Calm down, now, both of you. It's a fair request, Henry. Go get the box with the printed bills and let's check them. If we haven't lost any, there's a chance, just a chance that the government man said something

117

before he . . . before he died. Quigley was really angry about it. Why don't you check, Henry? Bring the box out here and we'll all take a look. Nothing like this has happened since Denver. But we must be sure—right, Pat?"

O'Reilly had put the Tranter back in its holster and nodded.

"Hell, I suppose so. It don't touch us nohow anyway. So there are a few bad bills floating around here. They could have come in from Denver damn easy."

"We just need to make sure," Kathleen said.

Henry sighed and went through the curtain into the back room. Quickly he returned with a metal container little bigger than a shoebox. He opened it and they looked inside at the bills, neatly stacked and banded in stacks of one hundred. Henry knew that there were four stacks of six, twenty-four packets altogether.

"Well, all the packets are here and in place," he said.

"So count each packet, I might have slipped one bill out each bunch."

"Did you?" Kathleen asked quietly.

"No, dammit!"

Henry picked up three or four of the bundles and tested them.

"They seem tight enough, and it doesn't look like they have been tampered with. Smudges would have shown up easily, and dirty hands would have left smears."

"So, you ain't gonna hang me after all?" O'Reilly said.

"The problem is now with the scare. Everyone in this end of Colorado is going to be watching for counterfeits. We won't be able to cash in any of them in case we need to. We might have to move before we want to."

"I need two more nights to finish that run on the Denver twenties," Henry said. "And I'm nowhere near ready with the etching on the new plates."

"We could be out of here within a week if we push it," she said.

"Wouldn't look good, our staying here so short a time," Henry said.

"Everyone knows that we're losing money," she countered. "But it would be nice if we could print the New Orleans order here too."

Pat O'Reilly marched up and down in the office, pulling the revolver out of his holster and pushing it back in.

"I'm just so damn glad you people trust me! Makes me feel all warm and happy!"

Kathleen shook her head. "Pat, don't get that Irish temper of yours all worked up. We simply had to know. It was as much to your advantage as ours to find out, to get it all out in the open and know what we need to do."

He smiled. "Oh, I didn't tell you, did I now? I caught a prowler in your house today, Miss Smith. He'd had the secretary open and I don't know if anything was missing or not."

She frowned. "Why didn't you tell me? Who was it?"

"Don't know who it was. Good-sized man who ran like a jackrabbit. I scattered some double-ought buck at him but missed. He ran back into town and I lost him in the alley somewhere. Didn't get a look at his face, but I think the jasper had a beard.''

"Two-thirds of the men in town have beards, Pat.''

"True. Maybe you better take a look and see if anything is missing.''

"Nothing is there that could hurt us. Nothing. No plates or drawings or inkings. Nothing.''

"Kind of makes you wonder, though, doesn't it, Kathleen, girl. First the big stranger and talk of a government man in town, then the counterfeit panic, and somebody prowling your house, and just now somebody took three shots at me at the back door, and missed.''

"But if that government man was that Spur McCoy, who is now planted in the graveyard, who was it in my house? Who shot at you?'' Kathleen's frown deepened.

"There could have been two government men here, working as a team, maybe,'' Henry said. "Or those Secret Service men may have followed us. They could put six or eight men in here.''

"Now hold it!'' Kathleen said. "We will not panic. We don't know for sure that *anyone* is on our trail. Let's just play it smart. First, Henry, put away the bills. Make sure nobody can find them.''

Henry vanished and came back a few minutes later.

"Second, we work tonight. We change plans and print the rest of the bills we need if we have to work all night. The paper will be late this week, mechanical breakdown. We should be ready to leave on a half hour's notice. Pat, you tell us which whorehouse or which saloon you're going to be in. If we need to ride out in a hurry, we won't have time to search every cathouse in town. Fair enough?''

Pat nodded.

"That damn colonel . . ." Pat said to himself.

"What?"

"In the saloon, that damn colonel with the Southern accent. He had a red beard, like you said that government man had, the one who got on the wrong end of them double-ought buck."

"I don't understand," Henry said.

"Damn right you don't, and neither do I." Pat added, "I never did actually see the dead body of that guy. Did either of you?'' They shook their heads.

"What I'm saying is this," Pat went on. "I'm not dead certain there was a human in that bed. Could have been some blankets, a damn *dummy!* Our government man, our Secret Service man just might not be as dead as we think he is."

Kathleen nodded. "The idea did occur to us. I talked to the sheriff yesterday. He said he'd take a look at the body, but he never contacted me. He's going to have to be more reliable if he wants to stay friends. We are tax-payers."

They all grinned.

"Damn, you suppose that Spur McCoy is still alive out there trying to find something on us?" Kathleen asked. "If he is, Pat, it's your job to eliminate him, and this time do the job right!"

CHAPTER ELEVEN

Spur unlocked the hotel door and stepped inside, then locked it again and put the room's straight-backed chair under the knob. Valerie had left the lamp burning low for him. He kicked out of his boots and pants, then the jacket and shirt, and slid into bed beside her.

She reached out her arms for him. "This time I heard you come in," she said. He rolled toward her under the light blanket and his hands found her. She was naked.

"I remembered how to dress tonight. Do you mind?"

His hands cupped her breasts, he kissed her and he told her he was glad.

"You found the man you were looking for?"

"Yes, and he found me. He might just decide he didn't kill Spur McCoy after all with that shotgun. He's a wanted felon, but I can't remember what he's wanted for." Spur put his arm around her and held her tightly. "Now, no more talk. Let's see if we can communicate without talking." She smiled and kissed him.

"I think you're beginning to learn how to play this game."

She pointed to the dresser which now held a bottle of wine, three kinds of cheese and two kinds of small crackers in a large bowl. He nodded. That would be for between.

Valerie Bainbridge rolled over on top of his long naked form and gurgled deep in her throat. She kissed him again and held his face with her hands.

"What does it mean, Spur, when I want to be with you all the time, when I want to touch you, to hold you, to have you touch me and to make love to me? I think about you almost all the time. What does that mean?"

"It means you're talking too much." He stopped her talk by kissing her and grinding his hips upward. She lifted away from him and pushed higher so her dangling breasts hung over his face. Slowly she lowered one at his mouth, which opened.

He licked and bit and chewed on the delicacy. She moaned in rapture.

"That is so exciting for me! It just makes my whole body start on fire and gets me so *wild*. I don't understand it, but I love it." She moved her other breast over him and lowered it to his waiting lips.

As Spur's lips closed around her breast he gave a low contented sigh. He was enjoying this woman too much. It would be simple to become serious about her, to take her back to St. Louis with him. She had been through enough. But he wasn't ready to settle down, his work wouldn't let him. She deserved a man who came home every night, who held her hand and made love to her and went to church with her on Sunday.

The surge of hot blood in his groin blasted all logical thought from his mind and he concentrated on the hot orb above him, wondering how it could enflame him so, how it could turn on his sex drive so quickly and completely, how it could knock out of his mind everything but the warm, pulsating, eager young naked woman above him.

He nibbled on the bright pinkness of the nipple. Her hips were moving against his, her soft furry patch trying to eat up his erection. He rolled her to one side and she pushed him flat, licking and nibbling on his nipples. Then her kisses worked lower and lower until she came to his hairy belly and his proud, male shaft.

"Would it be all right if I kissed him?" she asked, her eyes wide and bright.

He nodded.

She bent and her lips touched the enlarged, purple, throbbing head, and he jumped. She growled and kissed him again, then licked him and his hips jolted forward. She made more soft noises and then her mouth opened and she slid her lips around him and murmured, sucking as much of him into her warm, wet mouth as she could.

"Oh, baby, oh, yes, that *is* good!" he said, hardly knowing that he had spoken.

She came entirely away from him and looked up.

"It's all right?"

He nodded.

"I want to, I really want to!" She bent back and caught him and began working slowly back and forth on his throbbing staff.

A minute later he stopped her.

"Val, sweetheart, you know what's going to happen in just a little bit?"

She nodded. "Don't worry about me, just think about yourself and enjoy it. Darling, I've done this before—haven't you?"

He nodded. "But . . ."

She smiled and bent back over him again.

At once he was in a fantasy land. It had been so damn long since anyone had done this. He was seeing all sorts of wild and wonderful colors. The rainbow blazed and blossomed, the whole thing filling the sky. His hips began a small secondary motion, and she compensated and he felt his pressure building and building. He was like a giant steam engine that somebody had decided to build up and up and up until it exploded. The pressure was fantastic. He thought sure his skull would pop first. His hips moved now and she pressed him in farther and farther until her lips brushed his red pubic hairs. It was too much for him. His hips bucked and he pushed at her, his own spasms coming suddenly, quickly, and he muffled a yell as he emptied himself and dropped back panting. His arms were spread on the bed, his eyes closed; he was exhausted. She bent over him kissed his lips gently, then lay beside him cuddled next to his long frame, her arms across his chest protecting him from all harm.

Later he looked down at her, bent and kissed her mouth.

"You didn't have to do that."

"I know. I *wanted* to. I want to do everything for you, I'll do anything for you. I know it's not ladylike or

125

proper, but I'm in love with you, Spur McCoy. I never want to leave you!"

His arms came around her and held her then, and for a moment it was soft and perfect and neither of them wanted to move. Then the beautiful time was gone and she stirred and put his hand over her flattened breast. He petted her, one breast, then the other, almost as if he were seducing her. Valerie lay there smiling and panting, her face flushed now with the anticipation, her hands on his redhaired chest. He kissed her and his hand crept downward over her flat little belly and the mound where the soft brown hair began.

"Oh, yes, darling, right now, please—*right now!*"

He pushed lower, found the wetness and the small tender node and touched it twice, rubbing it back and forth. She shivered, then Valerie gasped and moaned low and long as her feet began to tremble; she gasped and an electric shock spasm shot through her whole body, shaking her, making her whimper in despair or joy, he couldn't tell which. When the spasm passed he touched the trigger again and played it like a banjo string and watched her build and build until she overflowed again in a great rattling spasm that left her panting and her hand grabbed his and pulled it away.

"No more, darling, or I'd die. Just let me rest a minute."

He kissed her, pulled the sheet and light blanket over them to ward off the coolness of the mile-high atmosphere and lay there thinking. It might not be so bad. He could request an assignment in Washington, D.C. He might get it. Or he could cut down on his field work. Grudgingly he admitted that he knew only one agent who was married and he had been married when he joined. He was on permanent assignment in Washington and had as his personal duty the security of the President.

Spur's arm circled her, pulled her close, and he decided he would face such problems if they came to them. Right now he was more interested in the matter at hand. She sighed once more and turned over and kissed him.''

"I don't know when I've ever been so happy, so contented, so very much in love."

She didn't give him time to respond. She kicked the covers off and sat up.

"Let's have some of that wine and cheese that I bought. When I get you drunk enough tonight, I just might ask you to marry me."

She didn't look at him, but handed him the wine bottle to uncork and laid out the crackers on a plate and cut slices of the white and yellow cheese for them.

For the next hour he told her about his early life. How he grew up in New York City where his father was a well-known merchant. He went to Boston to attend Harvard University and graduated in 1858. Then he spent two years in his father's business before volunteering for the Army, where he took a first lieutenant's commission and advanced to the rank of captain before the war was over. Then he went to Washington, D.C. as an aide to Senator Arthur B. Walton of New York, a long-time family friend.

"Then in 1865 the Secret Service Act was passed by Congress and Charles Spur McCoy was appointed one of the first U.S. Secret Service agents. I had inside help.

Since we were the only federal law enforcement agency at that time, we handled a wide range of problems, most of them far removed from our original duty to stop counterfeiting."

"When did you start traveling?"

"Almost at once. I was in Washington headquarters for six months, then I was transferred to the office in St. Louis where I had the job of handling all agency work west of the Mississippi. I found out they picked me because of the ten considered for the post I was the only one who could ride a horse well and I had won the service marksmanship contest. They figured I'd need both skills out here, and I have."

They nibbled on the cheese and crackers and sipped the wine, a rich burgundy from California.

"You understand that I don't want anyone else to know I'm a Secret Service agent. At least not until I've caught the group I'm trying to get."

She nodded. "Are you rested enough yet?" she asked, smiling.

He looked at her, slender, graceful and delightfully naked, and he knew he was plenty rested. He grinned. "I don't think you've ever been used up, have you? Ever been tired of making love?"

"Oh, a lady never tells. But we could try. I'd think five or six times would start to cool off my insistence."

Spur grabbed her and pushed her back on the big bed. "Lovely little lady, let's try for the record!"

They tried, but too much wine between 2 A.M. and 3 A.M. ruined their plans and they both fell asleep, exhausted and a little bit high from the grape.

CHAPTER TWELVE

The morning came softly, gradually, and Spur lay with his fingers laced together behind his head on the pillow. Valerie's head nestled against his side, one arm thrown over his chest. He breathed evenly not to awaken her. For a moment he was at peace. He had done a lot of charging around the West at the beck and call of the federal government. Perhaps it was time to slow down, to take a desk job back in Washington. This was so damn peaceful, so pleasant. It didn't feel like a quick night with a pretty girl. It felt . . . somehow more permanent, normal, satisfying.

He looked at her long black hair that cascaded around her shoulders, covering part of one breast. Beautiful. Spur realized again that he was more moved emotionally by this woman than any other he had ever known.

"Good morning," she said softly. "You were far, far away. I didn't know if I should disturb you or not. What were you thinking about?"

He looked at her, bent and kissed her mouth.

"Truthfully?"

"Yes, of course."

"I was thinking what a wonderful person you are, and how attached I'm becoming to you. And I was thinking that might not be a very good thing. I might walk in front of a bullet tomorrow and leave you suddenly."

"And I might get killed by a runaway horse this afternoon."

He kissed her again, then got out of bed.

"Some of us around here have work to do. I can't do anything at the newspaper plant until it gets dark, so I'll work the saloons. What I need is some proof, and so far I don't have any. Maybe in the saloons I can pick up some information or direction. If I weren't dead already I could storm into the newspaper plant and look around."

"Can I help? I could go down and ask for a job or something?"

"No. I don't want you involved because you might get hurt. Anyway, if they connect you to me, that ruins my place to sleep. As long as they don't make any tie between us, I can stay here."

"I'll go out and ask about Mort again, then. If he's back in town I want to find him. I still owe him."

"You be careful. He's probably an expert shot."

"So am I."

"Don't put him to a test."

She nodded. "I don't plan on doing anything stupid."

They had breakfast later in their room, and he put on a different disguise and darkened his beard with lamp black from a kit Valerie bought in the general store.

He looked in the mirror. His beard was blackish red, but it made him look much different. He put on the glasses again and a low-crowned, well-worn black hat. That helped more. At last he slipped into a black vest and tied a black string tie around his buttoned-up white shirt. He put a cigar in his mouth and decided he was set. As a final touch he took a walking cane.

"I may like this get-up so much I'll wear it all the time," he said.

Spur went into the same saloon, the Lucky Lady, where he had seen the bearded shotgunner before. Since the outlaw knew the apron there, it was probably his favorite. There was a well-used staircase to one side and six or seven girls circulating around the bar and the poker and faro tables. They all looked jaded and used, except one who told Spur her name was Ruthie.

"Ain't seen ya in here before," she said, leaning down and setting a mug of beer in front of Spur. The move allowed him to look down the front of her blouse at her surging breasts.

He glanced up at her, and she shrugged.

"So? A girl's got to toot her own horn around here. I know, I know. Too early in the morning. So come back later. My name's Ruthie, ask for me. I can make you feel awful damn good for only two dollars."

"That's more than a day's pay for me."

"So save your money."

She smiled and through the fancy paint she had an attractive face: clear blue eyes, dark lashes, high cheekbones and silky blonde hair that swirled around her waist. The dance-hall dress was off the shoulder and tight in the waist; it flared over her hips and stopped a scandalous six inches off the floor.

"You like what you see?" she said.

"Sure, doesn't everyone?"

"You getting nasty, buster?"

"No, no, not at all. Who wouldn't like a pretty girl like you, Ruthie?"

She took the dime for the nickle beer and he knew she wouldn't bring back his change.

"So come back and see me when you want to like me two dollars' worth. It won't break you. Come see me."

"Maybe this afternoon."

She put one hand on her hips and snorted. "Mister, I can't live on maybe."

"I'll be here, for sure," Spur said and hunched over his beer at the table in the darkest corner of the room.

For an hour he nursed his beer, watching the people who came in, the drifters, the bums, the down-and-outer panhandlers. Often they knew more about what happened in a small Western town than anyone else. But today no one was talking. Not a word was said about counterfeiting, or the government man who supposedly had been in town.

Spur wandered to the next saloon and had another beer in the corner, his back to the wall, moodily huddling over the mug, defying anyone to come close. But again he learned nothing. He was on his way to the third drinking emporium and gambling center when a small boy handed him a piece of paper. Spur ducked into the alley before he read it.

It said: "Meet me now, at the saddle shop." The signature at the bottom was simply "Cyrus." The deputy sheriff, the old timer who should *be* the sheriff. Spur came lurching out of the alley, piloting himself carefully along the sidewalk, down a block to the saddlemaker's delicious-smelling shop. Inside, Spur's drunk act fell away. Cyrus stood in the side of the small place where a half-breed Indian worked on a California saddle.

They nodded. The deputy waved him out the back door into the alley where they leaned against the wall in the warming sun.

"Didn't know for a minute if that was you," Cyrus said. "Black beard and all."

"Anything happening?"

"Yeah. No way I could talk the sheriff out of looking at the body, your body. He saw right away it wasn't you, but he didn't say a word. We went over what we knew: no identification on the body, and he was in your room, so we had to assume it was you and listed it that way. He was jumpy, angry about something. Back at the office he settled down at his desk. I went out on the street and couple of minutes later he left and marched straight down to the newspaper office. Sounds a little suspicious, now don't it?"

"Damn right." Spur kicked dirt in the alley for a moment. "Cyrus, looks like you're the only man in town I can trust. I think it's time I told you what's happening."

Spur outlined quickly his assignment, exactly who he was, and what he knew so far.

"Yeah, now a couple of things make more sense. Sheriff had a big meeting with the banker, Quigley, right after that counterfeit scare came yesterday—no, day

133

before. Seems to me the sheriff has more money lately. He don't complain how much the county is paying him anymore. I'd say he's getting a little something from the newspaper lady, and I don't mean her body.''

Spur nodded. ''Could be. What I need now is iron-bound proof that will stand up in any court. I need those plates and a batch of still-wet printed bills. I'm going to work the saloons again and see if I can hear anything. Then tonight I'll be at the old breaking-and-entering racket at the newspaper.''

''I'm on duty tonight. I'll make damn certain not to see you .''

'' 'Preciate that. Just keep your eyes open. If you see anything that could help me, let me know. I'll be around, and you know I'm not dead.''

''Yup. I heard that.'' Cyrus grinned and walked down the alley one way, and Spur went out the other. Five minutes later he was in another saloon.

It was nearly two that afternoon before Spur had worked his way back to the Lucky Lady saloon, the shotgunner's favorite haunt. Ruthie picked him up as soon as he walked through the batwing doors.

''Well, you did come back. You want a beer or a whiskey or something to rattle your balls a little?''

Spur grinned. ''You think you could do that?''

''I ain't never missed yet, Jasper. You want to be the first to resist me?''

''Bring me a beer?''

He started for his table but she scurried in front of him. She held up a nickel from her pocket.

''Here's that change I owed you from this morning.'' She put it down the cleavage of her bosom and stood, chest thrust out. "Why don't you go diving down in there and see what you find?"

He grabbed her arm and pulled her up close, then spoke softly. "Little whore, I know what I'd find down there. When I want a fuck I don't want to play games. Forget the beer, and get your little ass up the stairs. You hear?"

"You got the two dollars?"

"Hell, yes."

"Let's see it first. I don't want to have to walk all the way upstairs and find out you're broke."

Spur took a twenty-dollar double eagle gold piece from his pocket and let her look at it, then pushed it back.

Her eyes glinted. "How about the rest of the afternoon for that twenty? I do anything. Come on." She grabbed his arm and led him up the stairs. A couple of men hooted at her but she ignored them and kept going. Soon they were on the second floor and walking toward the back of the building. At the far corner room she stopped and pushed open the door. The place was larger than most cribs, fully eight feet square.

"You'll get your money's worth here, Bucco. How about ten dollars until six o'clock? I can wear you out five, six times between now and then." She reached some buttons in the back of the dress and when she undid them she pulled the bodice down, revealing her breasts. They were full, heavy, with dark brown areolas and tiny, darker-yet nipples.

"Well, you like them? Hey, you ain't one of them weird ones is you? I hate the weird stuff. But for ten dollars I'll do crazy things too."

He reached and caught a breast and rubbed it. "First some information. I saw a big guy in here the other day with a shotgun, full beard, black hair, work clothes, kind of dirty, and a nasty disposition. You know who he is?"

She laughed. "Yeah. What's it to you?"

"Another two dollars for his name."

"Shit, Bucco, I can't tell you Pat O'Reilly's name or he'd spread-eagle me and use his razor all over my body. You should know that."

"Take it out of the twenty."

"I will. Business first, big timer. Where's the gold?"

He took a five-dollar gold piece from his pocket and gave it to her. "I'll take your two dollar special, sweetheart."

"Yeah, figures. You can sit on the chair over there and get rid of your clothes. For two bucks the faster the better. Nothing fancy."

"Whatever you say." Spur sat on the chair, which seemed unusually solid. "Know anything more about Pat? Like what he does for a living, who he knows in town, how long he's been here?"

"Probably, but you only got one dollar credit, and them are all five-dollar questions. I could do you four for that double eagle."

"Forget it, I know most of it anyway."

She slithered out of the dress and stood watching him. Ruthie wore nothing under the dress but petticoats and was naked, soft, sleek and waiting. He bent to tug at his hard-to-get-off boot.

Later he knew he should have seen it coming. The chair was too permanent. The moment he bent forward to pull off his boot, the whole section of the floor the chair was on dropped away, fell straight down, then pivoted backward and away from him and he landed in a dark room one story below. He hit a pile of old blankets on top of a stack of hay. Spur was slightly bruised but unhurt. The trapdoor above swung quickly back in place, shutting out what little light there had been. Now he was in total darkness.

He stood and moved with his hands in front of him to the closest wall. It was scarcely three feet away. Then quickly he found the others. He was in a six-foot-square cell.

Spur wanted to shout and scream. He checked his holster and realized he didn't have his six-gun. Had it fallen out when he dropped through the ceiling, or did the girl take it from him? She had taken it. He was quiet then and pressed his ear to the boards all the way around the cell. On one side he could hear voices, but blurred, so he could not make out the words. Then he went around testing for how solid and strong the boards were. He found one side that was unmistakably the outer wall. The cell was built into the corner of a lower first-floor room. The whole thing had been a setup. His mistake was the twenty-dollar gold piece. She would probably kill him for the twenty. She had vamped him all the way from the very first. He was so interested in finding out more about the shotgunner that he hadn't even watched for the signs. He knew enough about San Francisco to know a shanghai job when he saw one. But what would they do with him now?

He found a weak point. It was perhaps some kind of

door, but if so it was well locked. He tested it with the heel of his boot. Yes, locked but not overly strong. Spur moved to the far side of the cell, clearing the way. Then he paced off two steps from the wall, moved back, took one step and jump-kicked straight forward with the heel of his boot. He was only just too close—his leg had not quite straightened out and locked when his heel and then sole hit the wall. There was a crashing sound, splintering jolt and Spur dropped to the floor. He stood and examined the results. There was no light coming through, but he found a hole a little bigger than foot size through what he guessed was half-inch siding. He reached through the hole, located a bolt across the wood and, after a minute of working it, pulled the bolt back and a door swung open. He couldn't see it, but he could feel it move. Gingerly he tested the floor outside the door. It was solid, firm. He stepped through the opening and again evaluated his prison. It was the rest of a larger room, perhaps twelve feet square, and he found a table, two chairs, and a dresser. But no bed. Quickly he went inside the cell and searched on hands and knees over the straw and old blankets, but nowhere could he find his six-gun. It was gone. He didn't have a hideout so he would have to make do.

Again he went over the walls, found the door, but when he tested the door knew it was locked. He tried his skeleton keys from the ring in his pocket, but none of them worked. He was in the process of working at the lock with a stiff piece of bendable wire when he heard noises outside. Footsteps came and stopped at the door. He stood, figured out which way the door would open and stood on the side so he would be behind it. The door would work as the only weapon at his command.

A key turned in the lock and the door came open slowly. A six-gun poked through the opening. There was some light now, just a sliver from the opened door. A lamp came closer and the light intensified. The door moved open more and he heard steps as someone moved through the door. He waited a moment more—*now!*

Spur lunged his two hundred pounds against the solid door, blasting it forward, ramming it into the man holding the gun, and the one just behind him with the lamp. Both men were knocked down. The gun exploded with one thundering shot, and the man with the lamp scrambled to his feet without letting the lamp fall. He surged into the room and now had a weapon of his own out and was pointing it at Spur.

"Here he is!" one said. "I got the sonofabitch in my sights, do I blast him?"

The other gunman came to his feet and covered Spur now as well. "Hell, no, not yet. We got business with him, remember?"

First they made him turn around slowly. He felt rawhide thongs bite into his wrists and kicked out hard behind him, caught a shin, but the six-gun in front of him cocked and he stopped.

"About one more move like that and you-all is one dead gent," the heavy voice in front said. Both men were young, miner-dressed and dirty with, unkempt hair and scraggly beards. Both had on soft billed caps unusual in the West.

The rawhide bound his wrists together in back of

him.

Talk is all he had left.

"What do you men want?" he asked.

"We sure as hell don't want that vamp Ruthie's iron crotch!" one of them said. They both laughed. When his hands were tied, the one behind him used a straight razor and slit the bottom of both Spur's pockets, catching whatever fell out. He found two double eagles, a small pocketknife, a few silver coins and some coppers.

"Well, now, I'd say this was a right fine day's work," the smaller of the two said. "Now the fun starts."

Spur had been looking at the smaller man and the fist into his stomach came as a surprise. He doubled over and staggered forward, determined not to go down. Spur had to gasp and stutter for breath. The larger man pulled him upright and slammed his fist into Spur's jaw, spinning him sideways. With no arms to throw out for balance Spur nearly fell again, banging into the wall which held him. The large man moved in quickly, pounding a left and a right into Spur's unprotected stomach, then a crashing right fist to Spur's jaw, and there was no chance he could keep his feet. He fell, skidding to the board floor, scraping his cheek. His head spun, his eyes blinked in and out of focus. His head lay on the boards.

When his eyes cleared he stared ahead at two boots. Each had fancy tooling on the sides, a mountain with a sunset in the back. The boot toe lifted his chin.

"I could stomp you to death in twenty seconds, drifter. You want that?"

Spur shook his head.

"Then tell us pronto who the hell you are, a name, a

home town, and what the hell you're doing in Durango.''

"Sam Grant," Spur said, "a rancher."

The toe rammed into his ribs.

"Rancher, huh? Where from? What are you doing here?"

"From Grand Junction. Looking for a lost brother."

The two men spoke in low tones for a moment. Then the same sunset boot hit him in the stomach.

"Why the hell you asking about Pat O'Reilly?"

"Old friend of mine. Thought I knew him from Denver."

"Fat chance. Pat don't got no friends. Think we better ask Pat to come over here and talk to you."

The other man objected. "Hail, what good that gonna do? We got all the cash he owns. What good it do us?"

"Pat has money, asshole. He said he'd give us twenty dollars if we caught anybody too interested in him, remember?"

"Yeah, yeah. I'll go see if I can find him."

"Get up!" the larger man demanded.

Spur struggled to his knees, then stood. The gunman was a little too close. Spur hung his head as if beaten, with no fight left. The smaller man left the room.

"That's right, drifter, just take it easy." The man moved his gun from one hand to the other and with it came Spur's chance. Spur lashed out his right foot, hit the left hand and spun the weapon into the corner. Spur kicked again with his left foot, slamming his hard-nosed boot into the man's right knee, shattering the kneecap, dropping the rouster in a spasm of pain. Spur

141

stepped back, and kicked once more at the man writhing in pain on the plank floor. His foot caught the side of the man's head and jolted him to one side, unconscious.

Spur had just reached for the .44 revolver that lay on the floor near the wall when he heard the ominous click of a hammer cocking. He stopped every motion, then turned to look at the door.

The smaller man stood there with a .44's black muzzle centered on Spur's back.

"Now we don't want you to get splattered all over the room here, stranger. So why don't you stay right where you are and spread those legs wide so nobody makes a mistake and shoots your bloody head off!"

CHAPTER THIRTEEN

Spur's hands were still tied behind his back as he looked up from the floor at the small man's revolver.

"Before today's over you're gonna wish you'd stomped old Gig plumb to death whilst you had the chance. He gonna be meaner than a sow bear with six cubs." He shook his head. "Lordy, this gonna be a picnic to watch. Now, you get on your belly flat out again. Gonna have to tie up your ankles since you so damned clever with them feet of yours."

He used more of the rawhide strips and then went to look at the unconscious man. He shook his head. "Lordy, you must have pounded him *hard,* he breathing but that's about all. I got to get him out of here and bring the doc. Now you stay put and don't so much as wiggle, or I'll pump about five lead slugs right through that ugly face of yours."

He holstered his weapon, then picked up the unconscious man and carried him out the door. Two minutes later he returned, closed the door and locked it. The lamp still burned on the chair.

Spur lay on his stomach trying to figure what he could do. He turned enough so he could get on his side, then brought his knees up and tried to roll over. It didn't work. He stretched them out again and from his side rolled over on his back, and as his elbow hit the floor he levered himself up to a sitting position. His pocketknife lay on the floor where the man had dropped it when he found the double eagles. Spur stared at it.

Possible, he decided, possible. He scooted that way, moved again, and when he was in the right spot he lay down on top of the knife, on his back, his fingers scratching for the blade.

He got it! His right hand closed around the small weapon and he tried to hold it so his left fingers could reach it. Each time it slid out of his fingers. After five minutes of trying with both hands, he held the knife in his right again and got his thumbnail firmly in the slot in the large blade. It was the easiest one to open. He rolled more on his side and held the knife only by the slotted blade and tried to open the blade by dragging the end of the handle on the floor. He tried again and again, but it wouldn't work. Too slippery. He let his hand fall against his leg.

Yes, that was it, some opposing force, some edge he could get some force against! He brought the handle against his leg and pulled on the blade. Slowly it came open a half inch, but his fingers slipped and he dropped it. Again he found the knife, caught it by the slot with his thumbnail and pulled the end of the handle against his leg.

It came open a little, then a little more, and he pushed his third finger in front of the blade to hold it as he got a better grip. He felt the blade bite into his finger but he held it, then pressured the handle more and the blade snapped open and clicked in place.

It was open.

He started sawing with the blade against the rawhide. He felt one string part, and then the blade seared his wrist, sinking into skin and flesh. He moved the knife, tested it to be sure it was against the rawhide, and sawed again. The tough band of rawhide leather parted. Again, again, then once more he cut the strands, and his hands were free. He brought them in front of him, sucked on the bloody place, then quickly cut loose his feet.

At first he couldn't believe it. The six-gun still lay where it had fallen, next to the wall. In his excitement over his friend, the outlaw had forgotten about it. Spur grabbed it, checked the weapon. It was a Remington single action Army revolver, a .44, and had five rounds in it. He looked around the room again and realized the gunman had left the lamp burning on the chair. Spur moved it and found his ring of keys in the hay, then went to work on the door lock. It took him longer than he expected and before he was done footsteps and voices sounded outside. He stood at the lock side of the door this time and as soon as the door opened he grabbed the person and yanked him into the room, then pulled the second one in as well. Neither one had guns out. The first man was the shorter of the two he first met in the room. The other was a tall, thin man in a derby hat and a red teamster's shirt. Spur held the gun on the small man and powered a right-handed fist into his stomach, knocking him to the floor. The second man dropped before Spur hit him.

"Questions," Spur said softly. "Who do you work for?"

The small one shrugged. "The owner, Lefty Larson. His place."

The other man nodded.

"The girl who suckers the mark into that chair?"

"She gets half," the second man said. Spur told them to tie each other's feet. Then Spur tied their wrists behind them.

"Who else is out there?"

"Just Larson," the tall one said.

"I need to have a little talk with him," Spur said. He opened the hall doorway and looked out. Two men stood ten feet down the hall toward the front of the saloon. One of them was Pat O'Reilly.

"Look out, Larson! He got loose again!" one of the men behind him yelled. Spur looked again and the hallway was empty. He saw a gun muzzle sticking out from a doorway. Spur aimed carefully and slammed a .44 slug into the molding beside the gun. He heard a scream of pain. At the same time he was up and running toward the back of the saloon. The hallway ended and he saw a door ahead.

Just as Spur slammed through the alley door, a gun boomed and a lead slug nicked the doorframe beside him. Then he was outside, into the alley, charging down to the first break in the stores, three buildings away. He looked back at a shout, but was around the corner of the dry goods store and running for Main Street. He got there before the followers made it around the last corner and he turned to the right. Soon he was lost in the afternoon wash of people who walked the Durango streets.

Spur had long since lost the cigar, walking stick, black glasses and low black hat. Now he shucked out of the black vest and pulled loose the tie which he sat on as he lowered himself into a chair in front of the general merchandise store. Spur folded his hands across his stomach and watched the direction from which he had come. His breathing had returned to normal by the time the two men came around the corner by the dry goods store and stopped. The pair talked a minute, then one went each way. It was O'Reilly who came his way. Spur watched him. The man walked slowly eyeing each person he met, looking down the street.

It wouldn't be long. Spur's right hand fell beside his leg, inches from the butt of his .44. It would be a simple, fast draw if he needed it.

Spur closed his eyes for a moment, then opened them and turned away from the man. O'Reilly was getting tired of the search. For all he knew his quarry had run the other way, could be out of town by now. But he came on. His glance slid by Spur, who wasn't looking at him, and then the gunman was past Spur staring at the men up the street. Ten yards farther on, O'Reilly turned and walked back, grumbling to himself as he did so. Spur watched him go with a touch of amusement.

Then he had it. O'Reilly—only the wanted poster called him *Mike* O'Reilly, and he was wanted on federal warrants for bank robbery, train robbery and the circu-

147

lation of counterfeit ten-dollar bills. Spur smiled. Now it fit even tighter. All he needed now was that bit of undeniable evidence, like caught in the act of printing counterfeits. That would do nicely.

Spur slipped the black vest from the chair and put it on, then fixed the string tie back in place and knotted it into a medium-sized bow and stood. He stretched, then ambled back toward the Mountain Lodge Hotel. He wondered what Valerie had been doing today. Why couldn't she just forget about that rawhider? As he thought about it he knew it was something he would never understand, the depth of outrage a woman feels when a man rapes her. It was a private and personal affair. She certainly was intense about it.

The moment Spur left her hotel room that morning, Valerie began getting ready. She had decided on a new approach. She would go to the sheriff first, then to the banker, and then to each of the barbershops in town. If this Sawtell had been around the area long someone would know him, and if he did live here—as she thought he might—she would have little trouble finding him through normal channels.

She put on her plain brown dress that buttoned to the throat and had cuffs at her wrists. Under the dress she wore her man's shirt and her pair of cut-down pants. She would be ready for any eventuality. First she went to the livery stable where Spur had quartered her horse. She had the livery man saddle it, and made sure she had two days of dry rations and a filled canteen on the saddle horn. Then she had the stable boy lead the mount to the center of town and tie it up at the hitching rack in front of the general store.

That done, she marched across the street to the sheriff's office and was let in immediately to see the elected official.

"Ma'am, it's a pleasure to meet you," Amos P. Hanshoe said. He liked the soft, pleasant look of this woman.

"Likewise, Sheriff. I'm hunting a man who owes my family money. I wonder if you have any records of a Mr. Sawtell."

The sheriff mulled the name around for a moment. "No, ma'am, can't say as I recollect the name." He called to a deputy in the jail to check the arrest records, but soon the deputy was back with the news.

"No one by that name has come to our attention recently, Mrs. Bainbridge," the sheriff said. "Is there any other way I might serve you?"

She shook her head and walked out. Across the street it took her slightly longer to gain an audience with Isaac Quigley at the bank. He consulted his files and shook his head.

"Mrs. Bainbridge, I'm afraid we have no records here for a Lawrence Sawtell."

She stood to leave.

"However, we might have a clue for you. We do have a Mr. Mortimer Sawtell. He's been in town for some time now. A respected member of our community. In fact he's also known as the Reverend Sawtell, since he's the pastor of the Grace Baptist church." Quigley smiled. "That's my church, and he's preaching most every Sunday now. He does do some traveling, and weekdays he's working in one of the mines. A fine, upstanding, God-fearing man. Now, Reverend Sawtell might have some kin by the name you're asking about. His church is right up the street and one block to the right. It's a residence now, but we're converting it just as fast as the Lord is providing.''

"Why, thank you, Mr. Quigley. I'm sure the reverend will be able to help me.'' She left the bank, her mouth set in a grim smile. That hypocrite! Leading his small congregation in services on Sundays, and then going on rampages of killing, looting and raping to blow off steam. Now she knew that she would kill him. She had to, to save his congregation from his double talking, double standard of hypocrisy!

She had to ask a small girl where the church was, then walked by it and around the block. When she came back she heard hymn singing and there were more than a dozen buggies and other rigs around the house. Some kind of service was going on. She touched the hard butt of the six-gun in her holster under the dress. It hardly showed at all.

When she opened the door she found herself in a small entry hall and a smiling young man nodded.

"Friend of the bride or the groom?'' he asked.

A wedding. Good, the preacher would be here. "The bride,'' she said, and she sat in the last row of chairs. The interior walls had been removed and shortened until fifty persons could sit in the combination dining and sitting room. The bridal couple was at the altar. She sat through the rest of the service, and when the bride and groom were kneeling in front of the preacher she had a good look at Reverend Sawtell. It was the same man who had raped her at the cabin. The same man who had shot her husband down without a thought. She wanted to draw and fire at that moment, but kept seated. She wouldn't spoil the wedding.

At last the bride and groom came walking quickly down the aisle and the piano player thumped away and everyone cheered. As soon as the couple was out the front door, Valerie drew the .44 and fired a shot through the roof. Everyone in the room turned, stopped talking and gawked at her.

She was on her feet moving forward, her weapon aimed directly at Mort Sawtell, who wore a black suit and a wide tie. His face was clean, his hair combed, but he was the same man. She moved so her back was at a wall and faced most of the people and the minister.

"Mortimer Sawtell, do you know me?" she asked.

Sawtell shook his head. "Forgive her, Father, for she knows not what she does."

She stared hard at him and he stopped talking. A nervous tic showed over his one eye.

"Mort Sawtell, seven days ago you murdered my husband in cold blood."

A cry of surprise and anger went up from the twenty people still in the church.

"No, no, he's a man of God!" one voice shouted.

"And after you shot my husband Ed Bainbridge, you raped me three times, then had me shot and left me for dead in my burning cabin."

"No, no, you've made a mistake!" someone called.

Sawtell had dropped his arms. His face was dissolving from his pasted-on expression of pious joy.

"Ask him!" Valerie shouted. "You women, look at him. He's as guilty as sin. Was he in town a week ago?

151

Was he here?''

"Yes!" someone shouted.

"No. No, he wasn't," a man said from near the front. "Pastor Sawtell was in Denver at a special convocation of our leadership."

"Denver, hell—he was loose with two other rawhiders, looting and killing and raping," Valerie said. She looked at a woman in the front row. "You, you in the blue dress. Ask Sawtell if he killed my husband."

The woman frowned; she was shocked and angered but most of her anger was directed at the accuser.

"Yes I will. Reverend Sawtell, were you at that Denver meeting?''

There was a moment of silence. Then Mortimer Sawtell, registered Baptist pastor and preacher of the gospel, slowly sank to his knees. Tears came from his eyes, his face cracked into shame and despair. Great sobs shook his body.

"Father, forgive me, for I have sinned."

"You sonofabitch!" the man who had defended him said. He jumped forward and kicked the preacher in the chest, bowling him over. Someone else started forward.

Valerie fired another round into the ceiling. All motion in the church stopped.

"No sir, no you don't!" she screamed. "He's mine, and I'm going to have the satisfaction of paying him back. An eye for an eye, the Bible says. An eye for an eye, a life for a life, and I'm gonna shoot him to pieces." She lowered the heavy .44 and tried to aim it. She was crying herself now, and her aim was off. The bullet plowed into the floor of the small platform at the front

152

of the room.

Sawtell jumped to his feet, roared in anger and darted out the back door before anyone could move and before Valerie could get off another shot.

She stood there stunned a moment, then she rushed out of the church after him. He was running, and she ran behind him. There were no saddle horses nearby, so he headed toward where there were some—downtown.

He beat her to Main Street by half a block and untied the first sturdy-looking saddled horse he saw. Someone shouted at him but he mounted and rode out of town to the south.

She never hesitated. She sent one shot at him but missed and kept running for her horse. When she got there she had the bodice of her dress unbuttoned. She put her pistol on the saddle and quickly whipped the brown dress over her head to the astonished gasps of three men sitting in front of the store. She dropped the dress, holstered her weapon, mounted the horse and wheeled away from the rail wearing her pants and shirt.

There was a shout of encouragement from behind her as the first people from the church ran into Main Street. Word traveled quickly and Sheriff Hanshoe came out of his office just after the woman rode down the street.

As she galloped, she pushed out the three spent shells and put four more rounds into the chambers, filling them up. She just might need that sixth round. She couldn't see her quarry ahead, but she could hear his horse's hoofbeats. She watched the ground, looking for the most recent shoe prints, but saw nothing unusual about them and rushed on.

The trail led into a thick stand of pine and Douglas fir, wound along the Animas River and into Ute Indian territory. She didn't know what state of mind the Utes were in these days. Valerie rode hard for another five minutes, then settled down to a ground-eating trot. Once she stopped and listened and heard his mount well ahead. At a high point she looked downriver, saw a small flock of birds lift out of some trees suddenly, and then just beyond the trees saw the man on the black horse, bareheaded, wearing his black suit. She guessed he was a quarter of a mile away. She took a chance, going down a steep slope, quartering it, saving a hundred yards, hitting the main trail unscarred, and charged on forward. If she could get within range of him she would shoot for the horse. She wasn't going to be softhearted now. Without a horse she had him. She would pay the owner for the mount if she killed it.

She rode hard now and felt her mare start to tire. But the push paid off and she came up on Sawtell quickly around another open spot just this side of a big swath of Engelmann spruce. He hadn't been watching behind, and now he turned. She had her pistol out and, holding it with both hands, fired twice. She was about forty yards from her enemy, too far for a pistol, but she automatically raised her sights as Spur had taught her, and after she fired she watched Sawtell. He yelled and grabbed his left arm, then fell forward over the horse and rode into the spruce.

She felt little emotion. She was doing what she wanted to do, what she must do. A soft smile lit her face

154

as she reloaded and rode. When she entered the spruce she slowed, watching the narrow trail, looking on both sides, wondering how soon he would fall out of the saddle.

Perhaps she could have this business over with and be back in the hotel before Spur came home.

But she didn't find Sawtell. The hoofprints showed plainly in the soft trail under the pines. She rushed forward, and at the end of the woods, a quarter of a mile on, she saw a grassy meadow a mile long, but there was no rider on the trail. She saw him nowhere. She stopped and looked back at the woods. He was somewhere in there. How could she find him?

Valerie turned her mount, patted her, and began walking slowly back into the spruce and lodgepole pine. Just past a three-foot-thick pine the voice took her by surprise.

"Far enough! Hold it right there, bitchy lady. I've got you in my sights and I reckon I'll have to kill you twice. One more move and you're a *dead* pretty lady! Now throw down your pistol and be goddamned careful about it!"

CHAPTER FOURTEEN

Her mind was working like a tornado. She couldn't see him, could see no gun. He hadn't been wearing a six-gun when he ran out of town, and there had been no way to get one. If he had any weapon it was a hideout, a derringer maybe, with a two-inch barrel, or some such inaccurate little weapon. It wouldn't shoot straight for twenty to thirty feet. He was off to her left somewhere. She sat there a moment before she drew her pistol and sent three fast rounds into the brush where she had heard him, then she galloped straight ahead.

There were no answering shots. He had been bluffing. Now she had to go back and find him. She reloaded carefully, eased the hammer down on the full chamber. She checked her belt loops. There were thirteen more rounds there. But in her saddlebag she had a full box of the .44 rounds. She turned the horse and angled through the comparatively underbrush-free strip of woods and rode back toward the area where she had heard Mort Sawtell. He wasn't behind the tree she guessed he had used. Nor did she see his horse. The animal wasn't hurt, surely he wouldn't abandon it. Then twenty yards in the back of the big tree she found horse droppings and bootprints. Sawtell had remounted and left. She followed the easy track of the animal out of the brush and back on the trail, picked up the hoofprints and looked ahead. A rider on a black mount was just entering the woods almost a mile in front of her.

She sighed. So he had a head start. He also had a bullet in his shoulder, no provisions, no shelter, and no extra warm clothing. She had all three. She set her mare to a canter toward the far end of the meadow. As she looked at the sun she realized it was nearly midday. There would be no food now. Later tonight if she hadn't found him by then. She kept on the move.

Valerie hesitated before entering the timber again. It was a mix of Douglas fir and lodgepole pine here, the firs towering over the smaller pine, and making a green carpet that marched up and over the lower hills to both left and right. The Animas River divided them with a curving liquid ribbon. This time she rode quickly into the wooded section of the trail, her eyes adjusted to the lowered light and she rode on with no more problems.

In a soft spot across the trail where a spring oozed nearby, she stopped and checked the ground the way Spur had taught her. It was simple to pick up the prints of the black here. She saw now that one of the rear shoes had been misshapen when it was made and looked more like a V than a U. She couldn't miss it. Then she looked closer at the ground, dropping to her knees as she touched a spot on a leaf near the shoe print. It was wet and sticky and red. Blood.

Good! she thought. Let him suffer. Suffer the way she had. For a moment the horror came back. Lying on the bed in the cabin she had helped build. Her legs spread apart and held that way as Sawtell knelt between her thighs, laughing as he rammed his fingers into her violated, already raw vagina. She shuddered remembering how he had laughed and squeezed her breasts until she screamed and then he lunged forward with his misshapen penis, jamming it into her, making her bellow with pain and rage. Only then had she fainted again and he did whatever he wanted to with her unconscious body.

"Good, you bastard. Suffer!" She said it out loud, then screamed it again into the forest, then got on her horse and rode hard. She checked her trail and knew she was gaining on him. She found horse droppings down the road and saw they were still so warm flies were not on them. A hundred yards after the trail forded the Animas at a shallow place, she found the horse. It was dead. One of her rounds had hit it in the neck and it must have bled to death. It lay sprawled on the trail, and leading away from it she saw the bootprints going directly into the brush, then coming out a hundred yards down the trail. Now the prints showed plainly, with the hard heels digging into the soil, and then the toes pushing harder. Spur had told her that was the print left by a person running. She tried it and the result was the same. Now she had him on the run.

She rode along the well-defined trail at a better pace, watching the footprints. At last the man had slowed to a walk, but still the stride was long and he was showing his strength.

The brush and fir closed around the trail again. The sun was moving across the sky. Now she had no hope of finding him before darkness. Perhaps she could spot a fire and move up on it. She would not have a fire. Spur had instructed her well on that score.

Then his prints vanished. They went into the brush and woods, but she could not track him there. An occasional bent frond of grass faded out and she had nothing. She led her horse back to the trail and rode a hundred yards in each direction. He might have doubled back, heading for town and a fresh horse to steal. No, he had as much to fear from his former congregation now as he did from her. He would go forward. She got back on the trail and a quarter of a mile ahead she picked up his tracks again. He was tired of crashing brush.

But he was farther ahead now. She rode hard for ten minutes, found the prints again and settled down to a canter. The trail wound around the crooked course of the river and fell into a canyon, and the walls closed in so there was only a narrow track beside the river. She let the horse find its way, picking along by the rushing waters, then edging along a shelf of rock where her uphill leg brushed the cliff. They came to a wider spot and she relaxed. It would be easier now for a half mile; then the gorge emptied out into a large valley.

She came around a small bend in the stream and the animal kicked a branch in the trail. At once a leaning log fell toward them.

She had time only to yelp and lunge off the horse and away from the falling log. She came off the horse feet first and went to her kees as she landed, but an inhuman scream of terror echoed down the canyon as the log hit the horse in the neck, drove the animal to the ground where it lay in thrashing, screeching death throes. She watched, horrified at the suffering the animal went through in its final moments, its head bent back at an unusual angle, its neck broken by the two-foot-thick log.

Sawtell! She grabbed her revolver and looked around. She saw nothing. Quickly she moved to the dead animal and lifted off her saddlebags which contained her stinker matches and food supply. She had let Sawtell get far enough ahead to find a spot where he could rig a deadfall. Spur had said little about them, but she had heard about them before. The log upright, leaning and delicately balanced so any small trigger on the ground could disturb the balance and bring the log toppling down on the unwary intruder. The branch had been the trigger in this case and placed so at least one of the horse's feet would brush it. She was lucky she had seen it coming out of the corner of her eye, or she might now lay crushed under the log along with the horse.

She moved silently with the saddlebags into some brush just off the trail and remained quiet. If Sawtell had set the trap chances were he would stay around to see how it worked. He would come back and might show himself so she could get a shot at him. He wouldn't know if she were hurt along with the horse.

Valerie lay in the brush for ten minutes, but saw no movement anywhere around the small cleared area. Perhaps he had gone on ahead, working away from her

160

as fast as he could.

She wondered what she should do. She could walk back to town and get there a little after dark. Or she could go ahead, try as best she could to track down the man on foot. He might figure she would go back, and suddenly she realized he was outwaiting her. He could see plainly that she was not crushed under the log, and he was too smart to give himself away. So she would put on an act for him. She stood, looked at the dead horse, and shook her head. Then stared longingly down the trail, turned and trudged back up the track toward Durango. She had to walk a quarter of a mile before she was back in the cover of the brush and timber. Then she paused beside a large lodgepole pine and watched her back trail. No one out there could see her in the shadows of the woods. Nothing stirred on the trail. She was in a position that she could see a half mile down the gorge.

At first she wasn't sure what it was. Something moved just beyond the place where her horse had died. Then the shadow moved again, stood and became a man. He shaded his eyes and looked up the trail for several seconds, then turned and began moving slowly down the path. She saw by his walk that he was limping. His left leg had been hurt, perhaps when his horse fell. She waited a moment, then slid out of the green and into the sun, out of sight of the figure below, and walked quickly down the trail, the heavy leather saddlebags slapping her back and chest as she moved. If she had full breasts it would be hurting her, but as it was she held her left shoulder out a little and hardly noticed the thump of the leather with each step.

Her mind was working as fast as her legs. She would try to move more quickly than he to make up time on him, and by the time it got dark she should be close. She would cover herself, not move through open places where he might spot her on his backtrail. Then when it got dark she would wait for his fire. She would get downwind of him and sniff right back up to his camp. Then she would kill him. Valerie set her lips in grim satisfaction.

The canteen she had taken off the saddle was heavy on her thigh. For a moment she thought of throwing it away. As long as he stuck to the river trail there would be plenty of water. But she held it. She did empty out the water, making it lighter to carry. When she left the river she would stop and fill the canteen.

For an hour she walked along the trail. Well past her dead horse she found his footprints again in a soft spot along the edge of the stream and at one place where the trail crossed the water. As much as possible she watched ahead and was careful to stay under cover whenever she could. She didn't want him setting up another deadfall for her to trip.

Ahead the gorge ended and it did empty into a valley, one nearly half a mile wide and three or four miles long. She saw a herd of elk grazing in the lush valley nearly waist high with soft green grass. She stayed in the fringe of trees along the river and waved at the big bull elk when he reared his head and shook his twenty-point rack at her. He was a smart animal—he had to be to live ten years out here.

Farther along, a white-tail doe left a feeder creek where she had been drinking and bounded away across the grass in twenty-foot leaps that carried her twelve feet into the air. What a beautiful valley! This was the spot where she wanted to come back some day and homestead. She bet that wheat, corn and barley would grow a hundred bushels per acre in here. It would be a great place to live, to raise a family. She grinned at that idea. First she had to have a husband and then get pregnant. Ed could never quite accomplish that job, and she didn't know if it were her fault or his. He said it was hers, but she wasn't sure. Men always said that. Now, with Spur McCoy it would be a delight to try to get pregnant! It would be a wild three or four months. She wondered how long he could keep making love once a day! Her aunt said that was a guaranteed way to get pregnant if it were possible at all for a couple to manage.

Before she knew it she was halfway through the valley and dusk was beginning to close in. She wanted some altitude to search for a fire or for some smoke. The closest way was to the left. She turned away from the river along a small creek that wandered that way. Halfway to the side of the valley she came to an easy-to-climb cottonwood tree. It could save her a long hike. She tried the low branches and worked higher and higher. Soon she was forty feet in the air and could see all of the valley. She rested in the crotch of two branches, slung the saddlebags over a limb and waited for sunset.

It came quickly and then the night closed in around her like a black velvet glove. Within a half hour she could see not more than twenty feet along the ground beside the tree.

163

As she sat there the strain and exertion of the day caught up with her and for half a second she dropped off to sleep. Her foot slipped off the branch and she slid a foot down the trunk of the tree before she caught hold again.

Valerie shook her head to clear out the moonbeams and stared up and down the length of the ribbon of darker-colored trees in the gloom ahead of her. She saw no fire. For a moment she thought of climbing higher, then shook her head. If she couldn't see a fire, she should be able to smell one. She tested the wind. At least half the valley should be downwind from her no matter which way the wind blew, since she was in the middle of it. The wind came from downstream. Good. That's where she guessed her quarry was, if he had stuck to the river. There was a town downstream somewhere, a small one, but a settlement. She guessed he would be heading there.

For another fifteen minutes she waited and watched, sniffing the air expectantly every now and then. Nothing.

Slowly she climbed down the tree with the saddlebags over her shoulder. Once the bags fell off and dropped ten feet and looped around a branch. She picked them up on the way past and soon was on the ground. Reluctantly she headed down the creek toward the Animas River again. There she turned downstream on the larger stream and had walked only a few hundred yards when a foreign, strangely out-of-place smell hit her nostrils.

"Smoke!" she said softly to herself. From downstream. She loosened the .44 in her holster and moved

164

as quietly as possible down the bank of the river. She had to cross one more feeder stream and got wet to the knees, but ahead she saw the faint glow of a fire. It was carefully shielded so almost no light came from it and had burned down to a mound of coals. She saw something being roasted on a spit over the coals.

A delicious smell of roast meat came to her. She moved with stealth, making no noise at all, going slowly from tree to tree until she could see the small camp. A man sat beside the fire, slowly turning a green stick spit held off the flames by two green forked sticks. Was he Sawtell? Who else would be out in this wilderness?

She brought up her revolver and with a double-handed aim concentrated on the second button on his suit. Then she lowered the pistol. She couldn't be sure it was Sawtell. To start blazing away at him made her no better than him or the other two. She had to know for sure. She moved closer, another ten feet, then there was nothing else to hide behind.

She brought up the weapon and aimed at the second button again. She was about twenty-five feet away. She couldn't miss at this distance. When she was ready, with her feet spread and her trigger finger tensed, she called out sharply.

"Sawtell! Don't move. Just relax. Nothing fast or you're dead. Now, turn around slowly and lay down on the ground, spread-eagled, way out—you understand me?"

"True I do, whoever you are, lady. But I don't think that guy behind you can figure it out."

"Don't try and bluff me again, Sawtell. Lay down and

don't move. I'm gonna tie you up and then figure out just how slow I can make you die."

As she finished saying it strong hands grabbed her from behind, and more hands jerked the six-gun away. She struggled and fought but the strong arms held her. Her gun was gone and someone ripped the saddlebags off her shoulder and then she twisted around, determined to find out who had captured her with so little effort. She saw the naked red bodies and the angry faces and she could say only one word.

"Indians!"

CHAPTER FIFTEEN

Valerie Bainbridge screamed at herself mentally. She was positively furious that she had been caught, even by Indians. They must have been following her for hours. She would not permit herself to faint. She had never been so close to any Indians, let alone these, who she guessed were Utes. She had no idea if they were friendly, angry, or little better than the rawhiders.

Slowly the men holding her released her until only one brave held her arm. He was naked to the waist where a pair of cut-off men's pants covered him. He held a bow and three arrows in one hand and motioned her toward the fire. The other warriors had seemed to vanish into the night. When they got to the fire, Mort Sawtell sat by the cooking meat. His hands and feet had been tired with rawhide strips and he glared at her and the Indians.

"Well, Valerie. That was your name, wasn't it?" Sawtell asked. "You've really got us in trouble this time. Do

167

you want the army ants to eat away your bare flesh when you're staked over their hill, or would you choose the rattlesnake with a rope around its tail that's attached to your leg?"

"I don't care much how you die, Sawtell. A preacher! You must have laughed at your flock's prayers and their worship. How long were you masquerading as a preacher anyway?"

The Indian who had brought Valerie in indicated she should sit on the grass near the fire. The blaze was built up and the rabbit over the fire taken off. When it cooled the Indian tore the small animal apart and handed a leg and thigh to Valerie, who sniffed it, then took a tentative bite of the hot meat and ate the rest of it quickly. The Indian devoured the rest of the cooked rabbit but offered none to the captive white man.

"Don't give up, Sawtell. If possible I'll talk the Indians into letting me watch you die. Then it doesn't matter what happens to me. I want to see you suffer for as long as your courage will hold out."

The Indian didn't seem to be watching either of them. He finished the rabbit, put the bones in the fire, then added more sticks.

When he cleared his throat they both looked at him.

"We have problem here," the Ute said in English. He smiled at them as they both showed surprise.

"You speak English very well," Valerie said.

He nodded. "Missionaries in Grand Junction thought they could make a farmer out of me. Ute braves are not grubbers in the ground!"

"You rape the missionary ladies before you left?" Sawtell asked.

The Indian hit him a sudden backhanded blow that sent Sawtell rolling backwards. He lay where he had fallen.

"Ute Indians are warriors and hunters. But we think it is strange that a woman chases a man. When the woman shoots better than the white man. When the woman tracks down the white man and counts coup and would have killed him already except for Standing Elk's quick hand."

"Standing Elk, that's you?" Valerie said.

He nodded.

"Yes, this is an unusual situation," she said. "Most white women don't try to kill men. But this is a strange case. Mr. Sawtell, Mort Sawtell lying there in the dirt, is a dangerously cruel, vile, murderous man. Let me tell you why I am wearing men's clothes, why I, a mere woman, have learned to shoot and to track and why I have hunted down this criminal and will execute him as soon as I can."

Five minutes later the Ute, Standing Elk, scowled when he watched Sawtell struggle to sit up. The fire was now kept at an even size by a young warrior who sat across from them. The other Utes were somewhere in the darkness.

Standing Elk walked back and forth in front of the fire. Valerie was not tied; she sat watching.

"This man-who-cries-like-a-squaw has done all these things?"

"Yes, Standing Elk. He shot my husband as if he were a bothersome fly."

"And he violated your body?"

"Yes, and then ordered me killed. I ask that you re-

169

lease him into my hands. That you allow me to continue what I had well along when you stopped me. I ask your permission to kill this obscenity, this devil masquerading in man's clothing?"

"In the town of Durango, he was a Baptist minister?"

"Yes, Standing Elk. He pretended to be. It's my guess that he killed the real minister more than two years ago, assumed his name and his identification and foisted himself off on the unsuspecting souls in Durango."

Standing Elk stared at Sawtell, who glared back at him.

"Come on, you goddamned savage. I ain't never asked for no quarter. Sure I done some things, man's got to live. But I ain't gonna grovel for a few more days. Hell, I've lived right well."

Standing Elk sat beside Valerie.

"Sawtell is a monster. If a Ute did what he does, we would banish him from the tribe, then we would hunt him like any other animal and castrate him, then we would chase him until he fell and died of his own evil."

"Good, excellent, Standing Elk. I had plans to do something much the same, with some refinements. I was going to use my trusty .44, if I can have it back."

Standing Elk watched her, staring hard at her large brown eyes that held steady on his in the flickering firelight.

"Warrior-Woman, you walk tall in the mind of Standing Elk. My braves watched with interest as you stalked, tracked and crept up on the prey. You have the heart of a Ute warrior. You have the Ute's cunning and ability to track and hunt. You have the mind of a roundeye woman who is wise, understanding, brave and deter-

170

mined beyond her years, far beyond what our people have seen before. The pistol you ask for is at your side. It has been there for the past many minutes. Only we two warriors are left here. The rest are sleeping, preparing for our annual hunt tomorrow when we will challenge the crafty bull elk you waved to today. It is a time for joy of the hunt, so our lodges may have food and hides for the coming months. Much meat will dry in the sun.''

She felt for the weapon, touched it and nodded to the Indian.

"Standing Elk, you are a great chief. May I offer some advice to the Ute nation?"

He nodded.

"Search for the honest white men to deal with. Struggle to bring your people into the white men's lodge, to learn his ways. Otherwise the Ute nation will be overwhelmed, reduced to a few mumbling squaws and wailing infants. The Ute nation must survive.''

"I will keep your words in my heart," he said. "As one warrior to another, I will not ask if you wish my assistance in your duties. Vengeance is mine, sayeth the Lord. But the Good Book also says an eye for an eye, a tooth for a tooth.''

He bowed ever so slightly, motioned to the young brave and they were gone into the blackness without making a sound.

Sawtell laughed from the edge of the shadows.

"You're a fucking Indian-lover too? I'll be damned.''

"You certainly will be damned, Mr. Sawtell. And that's something you may want to ponder over the next few hours. These are your last so I'd suggest you don't go to sleep and waste them. Sunrise is the best time for executions, I heard. My husband, Ed, used to tell me that. You remember Ed, don't you Sawtell? Remember how you shot him. Both shoulders and one knee as I remember—that was *before* you killed him. And then there's always the interest. On any loan there is always interest, Sawtell. You'll find out about that in the morning.''

She built up the fire with limbs she found nearby, took one blazing stick and checked the rawhide bindings on Sawtell. Both were tight and sure.

She had no intention of sleeping. She paced around the fire, then she built it up again and rolled Sawtell closer so she could check his hands behind his back without using a torch. He had not been trying to get free. Neither did he speak again. She hoped he was starting his trip into the hell of his own memories.

During the rest of the night she thought of many things, but mostly of her husband and their four years of marriage. It had been a good four years. She remembered that terrible day a week ago but tried to think beyond it. Spur had come as an angel straight from heaven. She knew she would have died of shock and heartbreak if he hadn't come.

Most of the week since then had been fine—glorious at times. She wondered if she could hold onto Spur McCoy. She didn't know, but she would try every way she knew how.

The first false dawn signals came and then the blush of light in the east and at last the stabbing rays of sunshine. Dawn.

She let the fire burn down and went to Sawtell. His

eyes were red-rimmed, his face a stone mask. She helped him stand, found a knife in his pocket and took it out. She helped him hobble to a tree where she set him down against it, then left and came back a few minutes later with a large rock and two stakes two feet long. She pounded one into the ground beside his legs, and used the ends of the rawhide ties around his legs to fasten his left foot securely to the stake. Then she cut the rawhide near the knot that bound his legs together and tied his right foot fast to the other stake which she drove into the ground four feet from the first. It spread his legs wide apart.

With the knife she cut the crotch out of his pants. He watched her, his eyes glazed, a little wild. She slapped him and he jolted bck to reality. He wore no underwear and his genitals hung there in the morning chill.

She took the kerchief from around her neck and tore it into three strips, tied them together, then looped the long piece around Sawtell's neck and knotted it firmly in back of the tree.

"Look down, Sawtell. Your privates. You have raped your last woman, terrified your last girl, you have brutalized your last whore in the cribs of the world. You are going to die painfully, and you are going to die this morning. Do you have anything to say?"

"Fuck you, bitch!" He tried to spit on her.

She had drawn the .44 and cocked it. She aimed carefully and fired. The round cut halfway through his limp penis, hit his right testicle and shattered it completely as the slug buried itself in the root system of the tree.

Sawtell screamed in rage and fury and then passed out.

173

She carried a handful of water from the river and threw it in his face. As he came back to consciousness he screamed again.

She shot him in the right shoulder.

She shot him in the left shoulder.

He fainted again.

It took her three trips this time to get enough water in his face to shock him back to consciousness.

"You're going to die, Sawtell. Die for all the men, women and children you've killed. You're going to die for all the women and girls you've raped. You're going to die because you raped me, Sawtell. Me, Valerie Bainbridge, and I vowed to find you and rid the earth of an animal like you. How does it feel to be on the other end of a .44 slug, Sawtell?"

His eyes rolled up at her and his hatred was a visual message she could read.

She shot him in the right knee.

Then she reloaded her weapon with rounds from her belt.

When the .44 was fully loaded again she watched Sawtell. He was still conscious.

She stood and fired five more rounds into his genitals until there was nothing but a mass of unrecognizable tissue and blood. She put the last .44 round through his forehead and watched his head thunk back against the tree. Then the blood and brains sprayed out on each side of the tree.

Valerie calmly reloaded the pistol again, put out the fire, picked up her saddlebags and began her walk back to Durango. The first half mile she sensed that someone was watching her. She was early enough that the elk hunt had not begun yet. She saw the elk grazing near the far side of the valley, as if they wanted to stay near the protection of the forest.

She was glad—a good number of the herd would get away. She knew the Indians would not kill off the whole herd. They would harvest selectively to preserve the food supply for next year.

As she walked she tried not to think of Mortimer Sawtell. She knew that it would be worse trying to sleep now. She was going to go on paying for years. But in time, it would heal. As she walked she felt clean again. She felt ready to go on with her life.

McCoy had been right about the paying, but he didn't know about the sense of justice that she felt. The sense that the slate had been wiped clean, the debt paid, and that she was free now, free to go and do whatever she wanted to with no regrets and no crushing guilt.

At the far end of the valley, as she entered the gorge, she saw a lone Indian beside the water. It was Standing Elk.

She came up to him and stopped, held her hands together in front of her and looked at him.

Standing Elk smiled. "A warrior should not be walking," he said. "A warrior woman should ride back into Durango as she came out, on a good horse." He made a motion with his hand and a young Indian boy ran out of the trees with a sturdy black mount with a saddle. At once she recognized the saddle and blanket that she had used when she left Durango.

"Standing Elk makes you a present, Mrs. Bainbridge. It is too far for so lovely a lady to walk."

"But . . . but . . . the saddle?"

175

"The horse that had it could use it no more." He smiled. "It fits nicely, don't you think?"

She smiled and nodded, her throat suddenly so filled with emotion that she couldn't talk. Tears rimmed her eyes, but she wiped them away.

He took the saddlebags from her shoulder and put them in place, then made a step out of his hands to help her mount.

The tears came then and she let them roll down her cheeks.

"Standing Elk, you are a great chief. The Utes are lucky to have you leading them." She unbuckled her gun belt and swung it over to him. "I won't have any more need for this. I did what I swore to do. I no longer *wish* to be a warrior woman." He took the belt and held it respectfully. She reached into the saddlebag and took out the box of .44 shells and gave it to him.

"Goodbye," he said.

"Goodbye, Standing Elk. And may only good times follow you and your people."

She turned and rode up the trail.

It was early afternoon when she arrived in Durango, left the horse at the livery and struggled toward her room in the Mountain Lodge Hotel.

As she expected, word had flashed through town that she was back, and Spur McCoy was waiting for her in the lobby.

CHAPTER SIXTEEN

Spur caught her arm as she stumbled. He held her up and more than a dozen people watched as he helped her up the steps to room 202 and walked with her inside. She dropped flat on the bed and gave a sigh of relief.

"I ache in every bone, I'm so tired I could sleep for a week, and please order me a bath and a dinner in that order."

"Soon. I suppose you know the town's been looking for you. The Baptist church has posted a reward for the capture and prosecution of Sawtell. Turned out he killed the real Reverend Sawtell and stole his credentials. The sheriff had a posse out until your trail went too deep into Ute country. Some of the Utes are downright unfriendly. And where the hell did you get an Army cavalry mount? He's got an Army identification number tattooed in his ear."

She lifted up and smiled weakly at him. "About the

horse. I thought he was an Army mount but I wasn't about to ask any questions. My horse was killed by a dead-fall, and after walking several miles I was ready to take anything. Haven't you ever heard that old saying, never look a gift horse in the mouth?''

''Who gave the horse to you? Where were you? What happened to Sawtell? Where's your gun and gunbelt? You didn't even have a hat.''

''Spur, old friend, lover and confidant. My bath. Please? Go down and arrange it and then sit guard outside the door. I'm about ready to die.''

She had her bath and by then a serving cart, courtesy of the hotel, sat outside her door loaded with fried chicken, fresh trout, three kinds of vegtables, whole potatoes and new peas in cheese sauce, breads and three kinds of desserts. She ate like food was going to be banished from the town after that meal.

Slowly and in stages she told him about her trip, glossed over the messier aspects of the demise of Sawtell and said she was never more glad to see civilization in her life.

''The Indian, who the hell was the Indian?''

''Oh, didn't I tell you? He was raised by some missionaries up in Grand Junction and his name is Standing Elk.''

''Standing Elk?'' Spur blurted. ''He's the wildest, bravest, most bloodthirsty chief the warlike Ute nation has! The Army has put a price of ten thousand dollars on his head!''

Valerie took a bite from a chicken drumstick, savoring the thick barbecue sauce. ''That really shows you how much the Army knows about Standing Elk. He's a fine man, he has concern for his people. He's kind and generous, and I have an idea that he keeps his word to the last letter."

She told him then in detail exactly what the big Indian did for her and Spur shook his head.

"It seems that stories just grow and grow once they get started. I figured Standing Elk had two ugly heads, six arms—each with an automatic rifle attached—and that his mouth was dripping blood from the roundeyes he ate for breakfast."

"Now, how is your little project going?" she asked.

He laughed. "It went to stop! for a while. Actually I was with the sheriff looking for you after the lay leader of the church came and told us what happened. We got back two hours after dark and I was worried and mad and decided to have a few beers and play a little poker and wait for you."

"So I'm back, and now you can get back to work again."

"Slave driver."

"You rode with the sheriff? Didn't he recognize you?"

"Nope. There were about twenty of us."

Valerie smiled. "And you were all worried about me?"

"And trying to find the killer."

"Have a piece of chicken," she said.

He finished the chicken, told her he had an appointment and slipped out the door. Spur wore old pants, a dirty shirt, a denim jacket and an old gray hat. His beard was still black, and he wondered if it would ever come out.

Spur got his horse from the livery and rode two blocks down from Main Street and waited under an aspen tree. Two ladies came from a house and walked down the street toward the business section. He waited. A third came out alone and he moved his horse toward her. He was in back and rode up to her suddenly, bent, grabbed her small form in one arm and bent her double across his legs, wheeled and rode hard out of town with the woman screaming at first, then laughing.

When they passed the last house she screeched at him.

"You can let me up now so I can ride regular!"

He slowed the black, then stopped, and she nimbly hooked one leg over the saddle and sat on it in front of him.

"Good afternoon, Ruthie."

She turned and looked at him. She lifted her brows.

"Oh, yeah, the tall one. I remember you. You caused all sorts of heck back at the saloon."

"Thanks for almost getting me killed."

"Forget it, all in a day's work." She looked at him. "Hey, you ain't mad? Jeez, usually all they do is rob the guys, take their guns and money and maybe ride them out of town a ways. I didn't know they was gonna do any more."

"You owe me, lady."

"Thanks. Nobody calls me lady. They used to. What the hell do I owe you, an all afternoon romp bareassed in the grass somewhere?"

"That and more. I want some information. How is the Lucky Lady owner, this Larson, tied in with the sheriff?"

"He'd kill me."

"I could do the same job lots quicker right out here."

"Shit!"

"True. What's the connection?"

"Not much. The sheriff gets twenty dollars a month to check the front door every night. A small kind of payoff."

"That's all?"

"All I know of."

"What about the newspaper? This gunman they have up there, Pat O'Reilly. What's the lash up there?"

"Better. Larson had been doing some work for them. I don't know what. He made some trips. He and Pat go way back. That's all I know."

They were a mile out of town now, south, and he found a tree that overlooked the river. He rode in.

"I like to get what I pay for, Ruthie. Do you mind working outside?"

"Hell, no. You can sell tickets if you want to. I used to work in this one place where they did sell tickets. It was in Arizona and I was called the 'last virgin in Tombstone.' Every night I got deflowered, but it cost three dollars to watch through peepholes. I had to fight just enough to make it look real. I got half the take and we did good. Three shows a night. Sometimes we sold sixty tickets and I made ninety dollars a night!"

"And you've been a virgin ever since."

"True."

They dismounted and sat down on the grass.

"Where's the blanket?"

"We'll have to use your dress."

181

She shook her head. "I better not take it off. We ain't that far out of town." She opened her bodice quickly and put his hands inside. "You need to get warmed up a little?"

Her breasts were firm and delightful. As he played with her she was squirming out of her drawers. She twirled them around one finger.

"You want to try to hit the hole, fella?"

He laughed and looked down as she spread her legs and flipped her skirts and petticoats up around her waist.

"You better not undress either, baby. Just open your pants and flip it into me."

"Now that's romantic," Spur said.

"What's romantic? You paid two dollars to get fucked, so I'm fucking you."

"Where did you get such a dirty mouth?"

"From my goddamned dirty customers."

"Figures," Spur said. He opened his pants and pulled his hard shaft out.

She shrugged. "Not bad. I've had bigger ones."

"Get on your hands and knees," Spur said.

"You mean it? Great, I love it that way."

Spur went to his knees behind her. He was breathing hard now, the wide open public place getting to him. He took one more look around, then pushed her skirts and petticoats up on her back and spread her soft buttocks with his hands. He found the spot and drove forward, impaling her as she shrieked with delight.

"I love it, I love it!" She turned and looked over her shoulder. "At work we don't have time to get inventive, know what I mean? We just pop fast and get to the

182

next one. This is more fun than I've had in months. And outside! Christ, it's been years since I've been banged outside.''

Spur had looked forward to this, to returning the favor to her, giving her something to worry about. But now the outdoors, the position he was in, the woman, everything crashed down on him and before he realized it he had climaxed, jolting the small girl flat on her stomach in the grass. He came away from her at once and buttoned up his fly.

She sat up and stared at him.

''Boy, I bet you ain't been had in months. You always that fast, cowboy?''

''Sometimes faster. Woman, listen to me. When I get you back to town, I want you to find Pat O'Reilly and tell him Diablo is here and I'm their new partner. He'll know what I mean. You tell him I'm cutting myself in on half of everything they have printed up. Either that or their whole operation goes up in smoke. Can you remember that?''

''Sure, you think I'm a dummy?''

''Repeat what I told you to say to him.''

She did, almost word for word.

''Fine, now get your drawers on, time I get you back to work. You've probably already missed dropping three or four gents through that fancy trap door of yours.''

''Yeah. I love to see the look of shock and surprise on their faces as they start down.''

''You've got a heart of gold, Ruthie. Pull them drawers up and let's ride. I've got work to do, too.''

They were back in town quickly, and Spur dropped

her off at the alley in back of the Lucky Lady saloon, then rode down and tied his horse in front of a small restaurant across from the *Durango News*. He went into the eatery and got a cup of coffee and a homemade doughnut, then sat at a window table and watched the newspaper office. For a half hour no one entered or left. then the lady editor, Kathleen Smith, left. A few minutes later the printer, the black man, came out with a stack of papers which he parceled out to a few of the stores where they were sold.

He wanted to down the rest of the coffee and try the newspaper's back door, but he wasn't sure that the gunman, O'Reilly, wasn't inside. He'd have to wait for dark again. He had just come out of the restuarant and started for the side door of the hotel when a ten-year-old boy called to him. He stopped, looked around and then frowned, remembering when this had happened before.

"Do you know Cyrus?" the boy asked.

"Yes."

"And are you over six feet tall?"

"Right again."

"Here, I have something for you."

The boy held out a piece of paper, but Spur grabbed his wrist instead of the paper and held on.

"Who hired you to give this to me?"

"I don't know his name. He's tall, too. He had a funny hat on, and a patch over one eye. I ain't never seen him around here before."

Spur let go, fished in his pocket for a quarter and gave it to the boy. The lad's eyes brightened and he ran for the general store.

Spur continued to the alley in back of the hotel and read the message there.

"Stranger. The sheriff knows you're alive. Have some interesting developments on our case. Meet me at 4 this afternoon at Plata #1 for all the details. They have something hidden in this worked-out mine, and if we can find it, should help everyone. The Plata mine #1 is just up the gorge to the north. A sign points off the main mine trail."

Spur looked at the name at the bottom. Cyrus. He wasn't sure if that's what the other signature looked like or not. It could be a setup, and if it were, Cyrus was in trouble. Either way he had to go and see.

CHAPTER SEVENTEEN

Spur checked his gunbelt. The cartridge loops were full. He settled his six-gun on his hip, swung onto the black he had rented from the livery to try to confuse folks, trotted around Main Street and picked up the main road that led north to the mines. He had gone about two miles when he saw the old sign that pointed to the left up a narrow gorge to Plata #1. He took the trail, left his horse tethered in a stand of aspen and lodgepole pines near a small stream and worked his way up the gorge slowly on foot. Less than 500 yards upstream he found the first buildings of the mine. It had been a large operation at one time, but now was crumbling under the harsh weather. He quietly checked two buildings, then headed for the open maw of the main tunnel against the side of the gorge. A bridge had been built across the stream which must have been a raging flood in the spring thaws. Now the bridge had been half swept away. He went across the creek on protruding rocks and edged up to the tunnel.

A scrawled note on a piece of paper flapped in the breeze where it had been nailed into the clay at the mine entrance.

"I'm inside," the printing read.

Spur frowned. It was looking more like a trap. But he had to check it out. If they used Cyrus's name they must know that he had contact. Spur shaded his eyes and looked in. A lantern burned twenty feet down the hole, and he could see another one on down the tunnel. He took a deep breath, drew his .44 and walked in. There was no one, nothing at the first lantern. He picked it up and carried it as he went to the second. Again no message, no body, no note. Spur stopped and as he did two shots came from the mouth of the tunnel. He dropped to the ground, rolled to one side of the hole and fired twice in return. Then there was nothing.

Before he could lift up and charge the entrance the whole mountain shook with a booming explosion. Rocks fell from the roof of the tunnel and then the light at the far end suddenly snuffed out and dust came boiling back toward Spur. He heard the roar of the landslide as what he guessed must be tons and tons of rock, shale, mud and dirt cascaded down the face of the gorge, plugging up the main tunnel to Plata #1 like a cork in a wine bottle. The problem was that he was inside the bottle.

Spur covered his face when a great gush of air surged into the tunnel from the entrance. When it subsided he saw that one of the lanterns had been blown out. He picked up the second one and walked back toward the entrance, but had to stop soon. Part of the tunnel had collapsed. He couldn't dig out through there in a year even if he had some tools. Spur took the lantern back to where he had found the second light and looked around. The main tunnel here had several branches off from it, some enlarged into "rooms" a dozen feet high where the precious silver ore had been removed. In one of these rooms he found what had been an inside office or headquarters of some kind. There was an old desk, two chairs and a cot. He looked at the cot again, and then heard the sounds.

Someone was stretched out and tied down there.

Spur flipped the blanket away and saw Cyrus staring upward at him, a gag around his mouth, his arms and legs tied to the frame of the small bed.

Spur cut him loose, took the gag out and waited a minute while the deputy sheriff got his dry mouth working.

"They blow up the entrance?" Cyrus asked.

Spur nodded.

"I don't know how they figured you'd come out here if they put my name on that note. They must have more spies. Somehow the sheriff is mixed up with the counterfeiters. But I don't know how."

As Spur listened he looked around the room. There was a shovel there and a broom, another lamp, and some old cable not worth salvaging.

"Cyrus, it doesn't matter one hell of a lot what they know or who is working with whom unless we can get out of here. Have you ever been in this mine before?"

"Nope. Not until half an hour ago when that Pat O'Reilly and two other dudes brought me up here at gunpoint."

188

"Do you know anything about silver mines? Is there any chance there's another tunnel that would come to the outside?"

"Damned if I know, Spur. I never did pay much attention to the talk. Me, I never liked being underground and I just shied away from it. Heard some guys once talking about how they was trapped and the only thing that saved them was an air shaft. I made up my mind right then to steer way around the mines."

"Yeah, I get that feeling myself. I've been in a few, but I don't like them. Can you walk? Let's see what we can find. We better use one lantern at a time to conserve our kerosense. Once those lamps go out, it's gonna be awful damn dark in here."

They went down the main tunnel for what Spur guessed was a quarter of a mile. The light rails in the center of the tube offered no help. The rails branched off into a second tunnel but it led to a dead end. At six or eight points along the way they had come to shafts that dropped away on one or the other side of the main tube. The shafts went down a long way, and Spur stopped tossing rocks down them. Back at the little headquarters room they rested a minute.

"You said something about air shafts before," Spur said. "What are they, shafts upward to the surface or outward to bring fresh air into the tunnels?"

The deputy nodded. "Near as I can remember. Sure as hell weren't any leading away from the main tunnel."

"The drifts, the cuts made on each side. One of them might have an air shaft. We've got to check them out. The only ones we need to look at would be those up

189

front here, closer to the surface. A quarter mile back in there it might be a half mile straight up to fresh air."

They checked out the drifts, each taking a lantern. An hour later both returned. There were no air shafts in the area.

"Come on," Spur said. "Blow out your lantern and bring that cable. There's one more chance."

They walked fifty yards to the first shaft, a square hole that dropped away into the bowels of the earth. Spur tossed a rock down it and it hit bottom surprisingly quick. He wrapped a quarter-inch cable around the lantern handle and lowered it down the shaft. Twelve feet below the shaft ended and they could see a tunnel and drifts working out from three sides of the shaft.

"Could be," Cyrus said.

"Might be," Spur agreed. "The main tunnel up here doesn't need an air shaft. It gets plenty of fresh air from the outside directly. The lower tunnels are the ones that need an air shaft."

Spur tied the cable around the mechanical rachet hoist arm and tugged it. The mechanism must have been used for hoisting four or five hundred pounds of silver ore upwards in a bucket or rail car of some kind. It would hold him. He left the lantern at the bottom, lit the other one for Cyrus and began lowering himself hand over hand into the twelve-foot pit.

At the rocky surface below, he untied the first lantern and waved at Cyrus. "I'm going to make a quick run down here. If I find anything promising, I'll be back. If not, I'll come and you can cimb down and help. We might have to walk through miles of tunnels, drifts and shafts here before we find an air shaft.''

Spur began his walk. Again he was on a small rail line. It would always lead him back to the shaft that led to the main tunnel. It was a beacon for him.

He walked one way for about two hundred yards, found dozens of drifts and vaulted rooms off the main stem, but no shaft to the surface. He went the other way and before he saw it he could *feel* the fresh air. He hurried, tripped over a rock fall from the ceiling and then hurried on.

Around a bend ahead he found the source of the fresh air. It was a shaft that went upward at a forty-five-degree angle. That made sense. Straight upward would mean a longer dig to the surface. He examined the shaft more closely. It went up from the side of the main tunnel, so work could be done on the air shaft and not bother ore going through on the tracks. The air shaft was not as big as the tunnels. It was less than three feet square. He put down the lantern and reached up inside the air shaft and pulled up his legs. By pressing his back against one side and his feet against the other, he could remain in place. Then by pushing upward with his back and lifting his feet, he could work upward and, he hoped, out. It looked as if the opening narrowed toward the top. At least it was a chance. He dropped down and hurried back to the connection of the shaft to the main tunnel.

Cyrus was waiting.

"Come on down, and bring the lantern. I found an air shaft."

Ten minutes later Cyrus stared upward into the shaft.

"It sure as hell gets to the outside, but is it large

enough up there?''

"Don't know. Hope it's like when you look down a long stretch of railroad tracks. Seems like the rails come together down a ways, but they don't.''

They looked at each other. "Don't say it, Cyrus. You might be able to get through, but since I'm bigger I might not. So I go first—it's what, maybe a hundred feet. If I make it I'll yell for you. All right?''

"Better than playing mole down here until we starve to death. I never did like rat stew.''

Spur began his climb upward. The first ten feet were the easiest. Then his back began to cramp, his legs muscles screamed and for a moment he was afraid he would go shooting down the slide to an extremely hard landing at the bottom. But he closed his eyes and demanded that his legs function, and slowly he edged upward. The closer he came to the top, the harder it became.

Cyrus kept shouting encouragement to him from the bottom. As Spur moved upward only inches at a time, he was aware that the shaft was becoming smaller and rougher. His back was rubbed raw in some places through his shirt.

But the reduced size worked to his advantage. He didn't have to stretch his legs so far to serve as brakes and it lessened the strain on his leg muscles.

"Getting smaller, as we figured,'' Spur called downward. "Looks like the diggers got tired, too. They must have dug from the bottom upward. But it looks like I'm going to have plenty of room to get out.''

He kept quiet then, drawing on some deep, inner source of strength to keep moving upward.

His right leg cramped and he screeched in pain. He

knew the only way he could get the cramp out was to rub it, but he couldn't reach his calf. He powered his left foot against the crumbly wall of the dirt shaft, and lifted his right foot and pointed his toe, forcing it outward. Gradually the knotted muscle relaxed and the grinding pain faded.

"Spur, what's happening?"

"Just a muscle cramp, I got it worked out." He looked upward. "I'm fifteen, maybe eighteen feet from the top. The air smells sweet and pure. But the going is getting rougher. The sides of the walls are weathered and I'm afraid there will be a rock fall or two, so be on your toes."

He worked rapidly upward then, without pause, sprinting as if he were in a race. He paused and rested, then set his jaw and worked upward faster again. Once more, one more surge like that and he should be able to get his hand over the lip, over the top.

He felt lightheaded at the prospect: he was near the end of the battle with his body and his mind and the damn air shaft. His mind clamped down hard again.

Idiot! Don't spoil it all now. Careful, don't grab something and let go with your back and legs and then have the handhold crumble or give way and send you sliding downward to crush yourself to death below.

He moved upward slower, felt his right hand touch the top, but he didn't look, he kept working upward. When the gentle afternoon breeze hit him in the face he looked and saw the hills, the sky and puffy clouds.

Cautiously he reached his hand forward, tested the lips of the shaft. It was solid. Firm rocks had been driven in place around the top. He thrust the other hand outward, then with a heave powered his torso over the lip of the shaft.

He had made it! He hung there for two minutes resting. Then he worked his legs out and shouted down the air shaft.

"I made it! Cyrus, I'm out, I made it. Don't come up. Let me get some rope or cable and you can climb up the cable. Hey, are you there?"

"Yes. Yes. Thank God you got up there. I had about given up hope."

"Hang on, I'll be right back."

Spur turned and looked at the surrounding land. For a moment he didn't know where he was. He thought he had moved one direction underground, but he had not. He found the stream, and the main gorge, then the creek that led off it. The main tunnel was over the lip of a small ridge. He ran that way and stopped, fading behind a Douglas fir. At the entrance to the mine there were ten horsemen. They were all working men, looked like miners on their way to town.

Spur charged down the hill shouting.

A half hour later the miners had tied together ropes from their saddles and some line they found in one of the buildings and hauled Cyrus out of the air shaft.

They all sat around, laughing and tipping a bottle someone had brought along.

They were miners all, and to rescue someone from a cave-in like this was a joy they seldom felt. They had defeated a mine! It was cause for a holiday.

Spur held up his hand and they looked at him.

"Men, I'd like you to keep this rescue a secret until tomorrow, if you would."

"Man, you're talking nonsense. We just saved a man's life. Even if he is a deputy sheriff, we want to celebrate."

"And you should, but if you celebrate too quickly, both of us might be dead. You see, this wasn't just a landslide. Somebody brought Cyrus out here and tied him up inside, then lured me inside the main entrance to rescue him. Then they dynamited the cliff so the entrance would be sealed. If we show up, or if the killers think we're still alive, they'll try again."

"You a lawman, too?" someone asked.

"Yes. But that's all I can tell you. You were on your way back to the mine, you say. Then with work tomorrow it shouldn't be too hard to keep our secret for a while. You do and I'll leave a pair of double eagles as credit for you at any saloon you name."

"Aye, let's do it, lads," one grizzled veteran said. They all agreed, and Spur and Cyrus began their walk back to town. It would be dark before they arrived, which was fine with both of them.

"I heard something you should know," Cyrus said. "They figured it didn't matter talking in front of me. The three men who brought me out were masked, but one of them was O'Reilly. I could tell by the way he talked."

"That figures."

"O'Reilly kept talking about the wagon, they had to get back and get the wagon ready. He said the shipment was all set, all they had to do was load the rig with enough furniture and household goods so it *looked* like somebody was sure enough moving."

"So the printing must be done, and they're shipping

195

the package of twenty-dollar bills out tomorrow. Since we're both dead, neither of us can be seen around town. But we've got to find out when the wagon is going to leave and who will be on it.''

They thought about it as they walked.

"What's the closest contact out of here where they have a stage?" Spur asked.

"Grand Junction, to the north.''

"Then let's make a camp just north of town, and tonight we'll go into town and get what we need to give that wagon a real surprise tomorrow morning. We can check out the wagon, which I'd guess will be near the newspaper office somewhere.''

"And I'm going to wake up the mayor and have a long talk with him about our elected sheriff.''

"Now we've got a general plan. We'll refine it more as we go along. First we stop the shipment, then move in and find the plates and get evidence on the three counterfeiters. Come on, Cyrus, let's shake a leg, we've got lots of work to do!''

CHAPTER EIGHTEEN

They walked to within a hundred yards of the first buildings of the town and watched. Each had specific duties. Cyrus was to get a length of rope, an axe and two good rifles.

Spur would visit the hardware store, going in the back door, and take delivery of a dozen sticks of dynamite and sundry lengths of fuse and dynamite caps. He also wanted to contact Valerie but he wasn't sure he should risk it. He would pick up two heavy blankets while at the hardware store, and check the printing plant and the newspaper office.

If things worked out right he could disable the wagon tonight. But he wasn't sure if that would only delay the trip and then not bring the counterfeit bills into his hands. He decided it would be better to attack them as planned out on the road. There was a light in the newspaper office front window and he saw the blinds pulled. He walked past but could see only one figure in the office, and he couldn't tell what was happening.

On a chance she might not be home, Spur walked past Kathleen Smith's house, and sure enough it was dark. He looked in the rear window and could make out nothing inside. He tried the back door and it was unlocked. Cautiously he slipped into the kitchen and was surprised. It was empty. There wasn't a stick of furniture, not a pot nor pan in the place. Miss Smith was moving. He wondered if she would be on the morning wagon for Grand Junction or if she would ride a horse.

Spur watched the back of the printing shop and saw lights there too, so there was no chance for him to get inside. He picked up his goods at the hardware store, paying cash for the two bundles, and carried them out to the little grove of aspen just off the north-bound trail they had selected for their campsite.

Cyrus wasn't back yet. Spur laid out the blankets, knowing they couldn't have a fire, and soon rolled up in the blanket with his six-gun in his hand.

His back still hurt like fire, but there was nothing he could do about that but forget it. By the stars it was just about midnight when Cyrus walked into camp giving the nighthawk call so Spur wouldn't shoot him.

He found Spur sitting on his blanket, waiting. Cyrus settled down with his blanket around him.

"We may have trouble. I talked to the mayor. It took some convincing but he called a meeting of the city council or aldermen or whatever the hell they call them now, and they voted to hold a committee of inquiry into the actions of the sheriff. I agreed to testify. But the word from the mayor is that the sheriff said he had to go to Grand Junction tomorrow to see about a prisoner being detained there."

"Sounds like the sheriff is going to give his friends a armed escort all the way to the stage," Spur said.

"That would tie him in tightly with the gang, but he might bring along another deputy or two and they could get hurt. They don't know how crooked the sheriff is."

Spur grinned. "Maybe we should slow down Sheriff Hanshoe a little. Who sleeps in the jail?"

"Just one deputy. He closes up at midnight and makes a round of the doors about one. Don't think we got any prisoners in there. Want to burn it down?"

"No, too much of a chance of burning down the whole town. But I do have a spare pair of dynamite sticks. Let's go open up the jail for public inspection."

They fixed the dynamite charge, cut a foot-long fuse which would burn a foot a minute and walked into town through the livery back lot and to the alley behind the jail. Spur set the two sticks under the joyce just over the pier block. They would blow the corner off the jail but not do a lot of damage. It should be violent enough to keep the sheriff in town the next day.

The two sticks went off with a surprisingly loud, cracking roar, breaking windows in two adjacent stores and shattering the rear quarter of the jail. By the time the deputy on duty and two sleepy saloon girls gathered to see the damage, Spur and Cyrus were back in their blankets.

They were up at dawn, getting ready. They had picked the spot they wanted a half mile out of town, where the trail that everyone called a road wound between boulders along the river and made a sudden turn into a narrow valley.

Spur planted the charges in the middle of the trail, covering them lightly with sand and dirt from the road so they were hard to see, impossible from back down the road. He and Cyrus would sit in the rocks and the moment the wagon got over one of the charges they would blast the three-stick-dynamite bundles with rifle fire. The newfangled explosive was highly susceptible to rifle fire and would explode almost every time when it was fired into.

They got the dynamite in place and perched in the rocks out of sight of the roadway but not more than fifty yards away. It would be like shooting fish in a barrel.

Spur hadn't figured out who would be along on the wagon, but he guessed the whole crew might come. Then he would have all the evidence he would need to convict them.

At 7 A.M. a rider from the north came toward town. One of his mounts' hoofs kicked a bundle of the dynamite, but it didn't go off. Cyrus hustled out to the road and covered it as it had been before. Spur hoped that no other wagons came through before the targeted one. He had taken a good look at it last night. It was a fancy one with regular wheels, but with a spring seat and red and white sideboards all painted with the name of the Barlow Freight Company. He'd never heard of it.

They waited another hour, then saw dust downtrail and watched. The rig came slowly, moving along as if it were loaded heavily. Two draft horses pulled the rig that was piled high with furniture. Spur guessed it was the furniture that belonged to the house where the editor had lived. The owner of the goods would be unhappy, to say the least.

It came closer and Spur saw that there was only one man on the wagon seat and one on a horse riding shotgun. The closer he got the better they could see him.

"That's Pat O'Reilly on the horse!" Cyrus said. He brought up his rifle and got ready to fire. "That bastard tried to kill me!''

"Not O'Reilly!'' Spur said sharply. "We'll get him later. First we stop the wagon.''

Cyrus gave him an angry look but nodded his agreement, and they waited for the wagon to straddle the dynamite charge. Spur saw that the horses hitched in tandem were at each side of the powder.

Both he and Cyrus fired at about the same time. Instantly the first package of dynamite exploded, shattering the wagon, dumping household goods everywhere. The horses ran off with only the wagon tongue dragging after them. Cyrus swung around aiming at Pat O'Reilly and fired. The round hit the horse in the head and it went down dead. O'Reilly scampered into the brush and with six-gun out. Spur ran after him around one side, and Cyrus went the other way.

Spur ran low with his six-gun out. He crossed the road and dodged two rounds of fire. Spur dove into the small ditch and lifted up, then ran for a boulder. There was no fire. He moved silently then, edging around the rock which was as big as a house. He lifted up and checked again. No Pat. He went around another rock and saw O'Reilly taking aim at Cyrus, who was in the open and looking the wrong way.

"Watch out!'' Spur bellowed and snapped off two quick rounds at O'Reilly. One slug caught him in the gun hand and spun the weapon away from him. The other arrived just as O'Reilly turned toward the sound and bored a neat, clean hole through the heart, exploding out his back and leaving a fist-sized hole.

They never did find the wagon driver. Spur and Cyrus picked up the unused dynamite, then searched the wreckage for the package. They looked in suitcases, inside books, went through boxes of women's clothes and kitchen utensils. At last they found the bills neatly bundled and buried in the flour bin of the kitchen supply cupboard. Spur packed the bills into one of the empty suitcases. They sat for a moment looking at the destruction, then got up and walked back toward town.

"It's not over yet, is it?" Cyrus asked.

"I can't prove these bills came off that press yet. I still have no real proof. Of course, now I only have to get proof against two."

"You want some help?"

"No. You go see the mayor, testify, nail Sheriff Hanshoe to the wall. One thing I really hate is a crooked lawman. Thanks, Cyrus. You more than earned your pay this week."

They entered the town separately, each carrying a rifle and a folded blanket, and Spur had the small suitcase. He went in the back door of the hotel and up to room 202.

Valerie opened it at his knock. She wore her pants and shirt and had her hair pushed up under her hat.

"Oh, good!" she whispered and ran into his arms.

He explained quickly what had happened.

"Now, I've got to get down to that newspaper office before they destroy the evidence I need. You stay here. I'll be back soon, one way or the other."

He reloaded his .44 and tossed the Winchester on the bed. Spur kissed her eager, open mouth and went out the door fast before he changed his mind.

The newspaper office looked the same. He decided to go in the back door, and to his surprise it was unlocked. The hinge creaked when he swung the door closed.

"Pat, that you?" a man's voice asked.

It was the printer, Spur decided. He pulled his six-gun, and when the black man came around a type case Spur put the muzzle in his right eye.

"You move one little finger and you're a dead man. And don't make a sound. Down on the floor, now—spread-eagle, *now*!"

Henry went down, but as he did he spilled a type tray. Spur tripped over it and when he came to his feet the black man was gone. Spur ran for the front and through the curtain.

Kathleen Smith sat at her desk putting papers into a leather briefcase.

"Going somewhere, Kathy?"

She looked at him, then squinted. She laughed.

"Land sakes, but you are a hard man to kill. Spur McCoy, isn't it? I cried the first time Pat said he'd killed you. I actually cried. You were so good at love-making. Then you kept popping up and I knew you were done for yesterday. I mean who comes back from a sealed-up mine?"

"Don't move your hands!" Spur said sharply.

"Really, you're afraid of a woman? I was only getting together some remembrances. I've sold the paper."

"I bet you have. What about the green ink and the plates for the Denver twenties? Have you sold those too?"

"What? I'm no good at riddles."

He kept the gun out. "The plates, lady. I want you to dig out the engravings you used to print the twenty-dollar bills."

"I really don't have the slightest . . ."

"I have the bills. Must be two hundred thousand dollars' worth. I also have the letter that was packed with them in the flour bin. New Orleans, as I remember the address."

Her expression changed. She was hard now, brittle, but still with the innocent poise.

"You found something. Fine. It has no connection with me."

"It was your furniture on the wagon, even your flour. That will be easy to prove. You might as well give me the plates. Pat O'Reilly is dead, he won't help you. And your printer right now is running away as fast as his legs will carry him."

"Wrong, you white bastard!" The curtain parted and a bottle came flying through. Too late Spur saw the sputtering, flaming wick stuck in the neck of the bottle. When it hit the floor the glass broke, the wick lit the liquid and it gushed into flames right in front of Spur, halfway across the office from the curtain.

Kathleen Smith screamed.

Spur looked at the flames. The woman was petrified with terror. She would sit right there screaming until she burned to ashes. He holstered his .44, leaped over the flames on the floor, grabbed Kathleen and sat her on the counter, then jumped over it and carried her outside.

"Fire! Fire!" he screamed. He heard the word repeated down the street. He rushed back into the office and into the printing plant. The back door was open. The black man was gone. He went to the office, found a bucket of water and threw it on the flames, but it did little good. He saw a blanket under the counter, jerked it and began smothering the flames. They were not doing much damage. Burning into the flooring, they did not attack the stacks of paper nearby. It was some kind of quick-burning cleaning liquid, probably what they used on the type. Three or four minutes later he had the fire out. When he went outside, the woman was not there.

Back in the office he began going through the drawers, examining the material in the briefcase she was saving. Nothing. He found no drawings, no zinc engravings, nothing to tie them to the paper money.

Spur moved to the back shop. Trial runs, the papers that printers always throw away before they get it just right. He dug into a square box filled with trash. Almost at the bottom of the three-foot-deep box he found a sheet of paper four bills wide and two bills long. It was one of the first press runs and in green ink that had everything on it but the red seal. This was what he needed. They would find the plates later. He stood up and grinned. Now he would arrest the woman and the black man if he could find them and stash them in the county jail.

"I don't know what you think you're going to do with that piece of printing, but whatever you're thinking, you're wrong."

He turned and saw Kathleen Smith ten feet away pointing a double-barreled shotgun at him. Both hammers were fully cocked and her finger was on the trigger.

CHAPTER NINETEEN

"Put down the gun, Kathleen," Spur said. "That isn't going to help you any. Prison won't be that hard for you."

Her finger tightened a little and Spur didn't think he could talk her out of it. He looked out of the corner of his eye for a place to dive. There wasn't one.

"Prison. I've been there before, remember? I promised myself I would never go back."

"What good will this do, Kathleen? Put the shotgun down."

"What good? I'll take you with me!" Her voice rose higher. "I'll take Spur McCoy, ace Secret Service man, along with me and I'll laugh from my nice warm spot in hell. Laugh at you because you didn't want to go!" Her voice went high, wild, and he knew she was going to do it.

There wouldn't be time or any cover. That damn scatter gun would shred everything in a twelve-foot circle. He saw her finger start to press the trigger and he dove toward a stack of heavy wooden boxes. He might have a chance.

Just as he left his feet a shot thundered in the print shop. Spur tensed for the thudding buckshot or double-ought buck, but none came. He completed his roll and looked out from behind the wooden boxes as another shot boomed into the echoing room. Then the shotgun went off, blowing a hole in the high roof, and Kathleen Smith pitched forward on her face and lay still, the shotgun falling out of her hands.

Spur jumped up and ran to the woman. He touched her temple where the large vein usually throbs, but it was still. Two bullets in her back had done it. He stared into the darkness.

Valerie Bainbridge walked into the light thrown by the night lantern. She still held her .44 and her face was grim. Neither of them said a word. She ran into his arms, tears streaming down her face, her weapon holstered, her fingers digging into his back.

"She was going to kill you! I couldn't let her do that."

Somebody raced in the front door, then through the curtain.

"Hey, where's the fire?"

"The fire's out, go call Cyrus Mercer," Spur said.

The man shrugged and left with his bucket, and Spur lifted Valerie's chin. He kissed her cheek.

"Thanks," he said and kissed her mouth. "Thanks for saving my life. There is not a chance that I could have lived through that hail of shotgun blasts, and she looked like she knew what she was doing. I owe you my *life*, young lady."

She kissed him back and smiled. "Then that kind of makes us even, doesn't it? But I'd like to try to take advantage of it for a week or so. I hope you'll stay here a while and comfort me."

"That might be arranged. But first we have to find those printing plates and any spare bills they had left over after trimming and counting them."

"Goddamn bushwackers!" a male voice bellowed from the darkness of the back of the press room. "Shot her in the back!" The booming sound of a handgun shot sent both Spur and Valerie ducking for the floor. Valerie groaned as they went down and Spur had out his .44.

"Oh, God, but that hurts!" she said.

He turned and looked at her.

"In my shoulder—get him!"

Spur waited without moving or making a sound. He heard something to the rear, he waited.

"Come on," the voice shouted. "Come and get me. Kathy couldn't take one of you with her, but I damn well will. Come on, you white bastards!"

"You've got nowhere to go, printer. The door is up on this side. You plan on making a break for it or starving to death?"

There was silence then. Spur heard more movement.

"I could burn the place down and get away in the confusion."

"Not a chance. I'd be watching that part of the building until it turned into ashes and shoot you the moment you stepped out of the fire."

"Then I guess I got to call you out, government man. Secret Service, I reckon. I'm calling you out for a shootout, a *walkdown shootout*! You know what that is, greenhorn!"

"Sure I know. Just one round in each weapon?"

"Agreed. Any time you're ready." There was a pause. "You give your word, white man?"

"Yes, I give you my word. Nobody will shoot you while we're getting ready. Nobody will help me. Your backup shooter is gone, you know that."

"Pat?"

"True, and we got the two hundred thousand in counterfeit."

"Damn!" A pause. "I'm coming out. I'm holding my weapon pointing at the sky. You do the same."

"Right. You can go out the door first. We'll walk down in the field due west of here. Is that all right with you?"

"Perfectly." He paused. "I never trusted no white man with my life before."

"There's one or two of us who are still honest," Spur said.

They watched as Henry came out of the gloom of the unlighted back of the room. His pistol was aimed at the roof. He watched them closely as he moved. He slid sideways past a stack of boxes filled with newsprint, hurried to the door and vanished outside.

"We'll never see him again," Valerie said.

"I think we will. Let me look at that shoulder."

"It's not good, but I can still come with you. I want to make sure he doesn't backshoot you."

"I don't think he will. He's been cheated and lied to, beaten, whipped and made to be a slave—he's taken so much rotten treatment from whites that he figured

209

printing up some paper money wasn't much of a crime. No, I think he's basically an honest man and will do what he says he will."

He helped her up, saw the raw pain on her face and walked her to the rear door. He went out first, looked around and saw half a dozen people at the front of the building. The black printer walked away from the structure, the gun not showing as he strode toward an open field to the rear.

Spur looked down at her. "Sure you want to come?"

"What's a walk-down?"

"It's a variation on a straight stand-up shootout. A little more control, and more deadly. Usually there are seconds like in dueling, but dueling is illegal now. Each man puts one round in his pistol. They stand an agreed-on distance from each other, say a hundred feet. Then they start walking toward each other as in a normal gunfight. But each man has only one shot. Either man may fire whenever he wants to. However, if he fires and misses he must either stop or continue walking ahead. The other man can then walk down to where the first duelist is, put the muzzle of his pistol to the opponent's chest or forehead and fire."

"That's terrible! I won't let you do it." She suddenly drew her revolver and started to bring it up toward the printer.

Spur took the weapon away from her and placed it on the ground, then they walked ahead.

"It's the kind of shootout where neither man wants to fire until he's deadly sure he can hit and kill the other man. A knock-down wound doesn't help. The other man can still get up and walk down to his opponent. It's the ultimate in a shootout and doesn't happen often. Few men have lived through more than one."

"But you don't have to! We could have dug him out of that building!"

"And you might have been shot again. No, I made the choice back there. Now I live or die with it."

"If he wins, what should I do?"

"If I'm dead, you send a report to my office. I've got an address in my gear. But first go to the doctor and get that shoulder patched up." He grinned at her. "Hell, woman, a man has to have some adventure, has to live out there on the dangerous edge sometimes. Half of the thrill of living is the danger of dying. The *risk* of dying, and the surging thrill when you beat the odds and go right on living! I didn't come all this way to die."

He saw that the other man had stopped ahead. They were a quarter of a mile from the town. No one had followed them. Valerie sank to the grass, tears close to overflowing.

Spur walked up to the black man cautiously. Both had weapons in their holsters. They faced each other from four feet.

"It doesn't have to come down to this. You'd get maybe five years as a first time offender. You spent more time than that as a slave under worse conditions."

"I'm not going to prison, one way or the other."

"Do you think you can out-shoot me?"

"Probably not. But my bank account in Denver ain't gonna do me no good in prison. My friends are both gone, only family I ever knew. I'll just have to take my chances."

"You insist on a walk-down?"

"Yes. After this is over one of us is gonna be dead, or so close to it that it won't matter none."

Spur sighed. "I don't enjoy doing this. Shooting a man in the heat of battle is one thing . . ."

"I been in one battle all my life, mister. Let's get on with it."

"Shall we take out our weapons and remove all but one round?"

Henry nodded, lifted his weapon cautiously as did Spur and together they opened the revolvers' loading gates to extract the fired and unfired cartridges. When one live round was left, they showed each other, tossed the other rounds on the ground and closed the weapons with the hammer on the chamber beside the one that would fire next. They looked at each other.

"For what it's worth, you three led us a merry chase. The agency has been looking for you for three years now."

Henry nodded. "We had a good operation. Too bad they sent somebody who was better than we were." His large brown eyes looked up at Spur's eyes and locked with him. "How far apart you want to be?"

"Fifty feet?"

"I don't plan to fire that far away, do you?"

"No, in this game you have to be sure of your shot."

They both nodded, then Henry held out his hand. "They call me Henry, I'd be obliged if you'd shake. I got nothing against you personally. It's just the way it's got to be. Whichever way, I can accept it."

They shook, then turned and walked away from each other. When Spur had taken fifteen steps he stopped and turned. Henry was already facing him. They were a little over sixty feet apart. Twenty yards—it wasn't impossible, but the percentages were too low.

As he walked out he had steeled himself to draw at once and wait until he was at the twenty-foot mark before he fired. Spur would draw and aim and perhaps fluster Henry, who may have never shot at another human being more than once or twice.

"Ready?" Spur asked, his voice unusually calm.

Henry nodded and they started walking toward each other. They took slow deliberate steps and both had out their weapons.

Spur had heard hours of discussion about the best way to live through a walk-down, and each time the rule came out to shoot first and kill, not to wait for the other man to have a chance to kill you. *To shoot first and kill!*

Those thoughts drilled into his brain as he walked slowly toward Henry. His mind was slashing at a hundred thoughts, brushing past them, all the time counting down the distance.

Fifty-five feet.

How good could Henry be since he wasn't a gunfighter?

Should we wait past twenty feet? Where would Henry choose to fire? Did he have a set distance picked out or would he become frightened and emotional and fire on impulse?

Fifty feet.

It had to be a chest shot, biggest target, most vital spots to hit, a heart shot. What would Henry try for? When would the man shoot? Just don't miss! A kill shot the first try. Damn, the waiting, the goddamn suspense, the waiting. He took another slow step.

He had to fire before Henry turned sideways in the classic duelist's defense. A shoulder hit would not do the job. Under the arm and through the heart would, but that was a tough target.

Forty-five feet.

His stare never left the black face. What could he read there? Nervousness, a slight tremor? He looked at the weapon: a Colt, an older one, but heavy, accurate. God, right now he wished he had refused the walk-down. Who would have known? He should have blasted him out of there. Tricked him, burned him out, anything but this. This was stupid!

Forty feet.

Maybe he should fire earlier, go for a lucky shot? No, dammit, he decided once. Twenty feet, that was it.

Thirty-five feet.

Suddenly he was calm. He knew precisely what he had to do, exactly how he would do it. He would lift his arm at twenty-five feet, stop and take a spread-legged stance, bend his knees and use both hands to hold the weapon.

Thirty feet.

Henry brought up his weapon and kept walking. Spur lifted the Colt .44 and took three more steps, then he bent, flexed his knees, grasped the Colt handle with both his hands and brought the sights down to center on the blue shirt over the black chest.

He squeezed the trigger, watching for any last-minute lurch or dive by Henry. There was none. The weapon went off and the recoil pushed it above his head as he watched through his arms as the bullet slammed into Henry's chest, drove him back a step, but did not knock him down.

Spur watched with amazement as the black man's face turned from pain into a triumphant smile. He lifted his weapon again and took a step forward, then another one.

"Noooooooooooo!" A scream of rage razored through the calm morning air, and Valerie repeated it as she ran forward, both hands held high in defiance, in tormented fury.

Spur didn't look at her. All he could see was the small black man with the big .44 taking another step toward him.

CHAPTER TWENTY

Spur remained exactly where he was. His arms had come down to his side; he still stood with legs spread in his shooting stance. Henry took another step, his expression changing from a smile to one of surprise and then strain. His arm with the gun began to lower slowly. Then he screamed. The cry of pain ended in a red frothy gurgle as blood spewed from his mouth. His finger jerked on the trigger; the .44 bullet slammed into the ground almost at his feet. His eyes glazed and then rolled up in his head until Spur could see only white. He vomited bright red blood that gushed out of him again and again. His legs seemed to disobey him.

One leg tried to go sideways. The other one buckled, throwing him forward to one shoulder where he hit hard, rolled over and lay on his face in the field.

Spur's body came unfrozen. Slowly he put the empty six-gun back in the holster and turned toward Valerie. She had stopped, staring in amazement at the body only a few yards from her. The terror and anguish on her face dissolved into a marvelous smile and she rushed to Spur and held him, her arms wrapped around him so fiercely, so tightly that he wondered if she would ever let go. He picked her up and carried her, walking slowly back toward the rear of the newspaper office.

A stream of men and a few women headed toward them. One man broke from the pack and ran hard, coming ahead of the rest. He arrived first and Spur nodded.

"How did it go with the sheriff, Cyrus?" Spur asked.

Cyrus frowned and looked at the dead man. "Went well, Spur. Went well. Henry dead?"

"True. He challenged me to a walk-down. Sort of thing a man can't very well back off from."

"A walk-down! Christ, glad you're alive. You shoot first!"

"Yep." They walked again, back toward the newspaper.

"You find Kathleen?"

"Fact is we did. Have to be a hearing, you know that. We got law in this town. Leastwise now we do. Hanshoe is in jail. I'm the new interim and acting sheriff. Plan on running for the office when it comes up in September."

"Good, you'll be elected. Lots of folks around here know you, Cyrus." Spur set Valerie down, then held the door for her to go into the newspaper office.

Two men were taking the big body of Kathleen Smith out the front door on a stretcher.

Spur looked at Cyrus. "Appreciate it if we could lock both doors, Sheriff. I still have to find the plates they printed those bills from. The agency is going to want

217

them.''

Cyrus pointed to a man who had come into the building with them, and the deputy went to the front door and they heard it lock.

Spur looked around the big room. ''Somewhere in here are two zinc etchings, exactly the same size of those U.S. notes.''

Cyrus nodded. ''I'll send you two men to help, Spur. I best be getting back to the office and getting the new way of doing things into the works.''

Spur waved as he began to section off the big room. They would work one part of it at a time, from floor to rafters. Nothing would be overlooked.

It was nearly six hours later when they found the second and last zinc engraving of the twenty-dollar bill. The first one had been taped to the underside of the large frame of the flatbed press. The last one was in an envelope in a box full of old statements and bills, on the bottom of a stack. The plates evidently were the last item Kathleen planned to pick up before they left by buggy that noon. The rig had been rented from the livery and sat in back waiting for them.

With the plates and the counterfeit bills, Spur went to the sheriff's office and made out his reports.

Cyrus sat behind the desk, looking slightly uncomfortable.

''Appreciate your coming in and clearing the decks this way, McCoy. Know it's a passle of trouble for you, but you'll have all the facts well in hand to make out your own reports to your company.''

''True,'' Spur said. He had filled out a complaint charging the three with counterfeiting, then reported the resistance and the demise of each and the recovery of the bogus bills and the plates. It was all wrapped up neatly and it would look good on Cyrus's record when election came up.

"About these other two deaths, Spur. Sure would like to get them off the books. One was a gent named Chug Rollins."

Spur hesitated. Hell, why not?

He told the sheriff how he had come on the woman's homestead, what happened, and how she identified the rapist to Spur.

"When I went to apprehend the law violator, he produced a weapon and I was obliged to return fire. I couldn't report it at the time since it might compromise my investigation of the counterfeiting."

Cyrus nodded. "Sounds reasonable. Write that out for me and we can close that one." He looked through his papers a minute.

"We have just one more you could help me with. Gent by the name of Mort Sawtell, leastwise that's the name he was going by. Seems he was a rawhider who probably killed the real Reverend Sawtell and took his identification. He was chased out of town by one Valerie Bainbridge, and he hasn't been seen since. The local Baptist congregation would be ever so pleased if they knew that the killing of their pastor had been avenged."

Spur laughed. "You trying to clear up every case in the county in the last twenty years?"

"No, Spur, just since you arrived in town. I'll take care of the gent on the road this morning. What about Sawtell?"

Spur took pen and paper and wrote this report.

"Being a federal law enforcement office, I give this deposition in the case of one Mortimer Sawtell, a false name. Sawtell was involved in the slaying of Ed Bainbridge on this month the 24th day, and was pursued to Durango, where he was at last identified by the deceased man's widow, who then chased him into Ute territory. It is the sworn testimony of the widow that the said Mort Sawtell did fall from his horse in the Ute Indian territories, and in this fall did break his neck and expire."

Spur stood up and watched Cyrus read his statement.

"Well, now, Spur, looks like that should take care of everything. The mayor has a little reception tonight, and he asked me to be sure and have you come. There's going to be plenty of sippin' whiskey, and refreshments at the town meeting house."

Spur laughed and looked out the window.

"Now, Sheriff, that's one thing the Agency frowns on, messing in local politics. Fact is I have a big evening planned. Then I also have to get my report written and bundle up all this evidence to ship back to the home office. Going to be a busy time."

Cyrus stood and held out his hand. "Hell, I know how that is. I wouldn't be going myself if I didn't really want this job. We got Hanshoe in jail right now, but he'll probably get out on bail soon as the judge gets here next week. Hanshoe is charged with several felony counts including conspiracy to produce counterfeit U.S. bank notes. We've got enough evidence on him to at least get him removed from office."

"Good. Now I better let you get on with the rest of

220

your important duties." Spur grinned and swung out of the jailhouse door feeling better than he had in a week.

Back at the hotel, Valerie answered his knock and let him in. She wore a sparkling new blue dress that was cut low across the bodice, with small puff sleeves and pulled in sharply at the waist. He had given her twenty dollars to go on a shopping spree.

"Like it? I had a bath and everything. I ordered supper sent up just as soon as you arrived. I hope you don't mind."

He kissed her gently, then kissed her again and his open mouth met hers and their tongues fought for a minute.

She pulled away and answered a knock at the door. "Enough of that, we've got all night. First I want you fed right up to the top."

The waiter brought in the rolling tray of food including rare T-bone steaks, four vegtables, three kinds of sweet rolls and a table full of other food, including cherry pie, chocolate pudding and a light angelfood cake.

"I fully intend to eat until I'm too full to move," Spur said.

Valerie grinned and held out a chair for him.

Two hours later they pushed the serving table away and fell on the bed exhausted and full. She rolled over and kissed him.

"You know, for almost two days I was trying to decide how to trap you, how to convince you that you should give up this wild, dangerous, romantic life of a super sheriff, masterful marshal, and settle down with me in my bed. But then I decided against that because I realized I couldn't compete with the whole western two-thirds of the continent. Impossible. So I figured I'd shoot for second best. What I'm suggesting is that you need four days here in Durango to settle down, to get your reports written and to rest up before you go back to Grand Junction where the stage comes. All I ask is that you stay here with me, and that you enjoy yourself, and that you make love to me at least three times a day."

He kissed her, pulled her on top of him and reached up to kiss both her breasts.

"Tell you what. How about five days instead of four? I want you to show me that perfect valley you saw with the elk and the Utes in it. Then I'll be ready to go. And maybe we better start off making love twice a day."

He sat up suddenly. "Hey, your shoulder. Did you go see the doctor? How is it? What did he do? Let me see it."

She pushed the dress off her left shoulder and showed him the bandage.

"The bullet missed the bone, so it isn't as bad as it felt. I thought sure he had killed me. The doctor got the bullet out as I screamed, and then he gave me a drink of brandy and put some powder and two kinds of liquids on it and wrapped it all up and said I should come back in two days." She grinned. "I can lift it and everything." She didn't move the dress back on her shoulder. He unbuttoned the front and reached past the tops of the petticoats and the silken chemise and closed his hand around her breast.

222

"Oh, yes, that feels good," she said. "Kind of natural and normal and wishing it would happen often."

"For the next five days it will." He kissed her and then leaned back.

"You're right, Valerie. It does feel good, kind of natural and normal." He reached in his shirt pocket and took out an envelope. "I lied a little today. I told the sheriff how you chased Sawtell into Indian country and there he fell off his horse and broke his neck. He told me that there was a reward out for Sawtell by the local church of a hundred dollars. This is a bank draft in that amount. They want you to keep it. They know you suffered more at his hands than they did."

"A hundred dollars! I could go back to Denver."

"You could." He handed her another envelope. "Then you remember that gold dust you and Ed worked so hard panning? The sheriff found the jar in Chug's room and was holding it. I convinced the new sheriff it was yours. The dust had been weighed and banked and here is a bank draft for what it was worth. Gold sells for twenty dollars and sixty-seven cents an ounce, and the sheriff said you had a little over thirty-two ounces, so the check is for six hundred sixty-one dollars and forty-eight cents."

She looked at him with her mouth hanging open.

"I thought . . ." She hunched her shoulders. "Figured that was just lost and gone, with all the rest of it. I never . . ." She blinked back tears and kissed him, moved his hands to help her with the dress.

"Darling Spur, I'll never know . . ." She took a long, deep sigh. "Right now I just want to feel you on me and inside me and just everywhere!"

It was almost 3 A.M. when Valerie bounced up from the bed beside him.

"That's enough rest, let's open a new bottle of wine and do something unusual for number four. I suddenly feel wild and brave." She grinned. "You've done a lot more of this sort of thing than I have, Mr. McCoy. Come and give me a lesson, show me how the Indian girls make love. Or maybe the hot-blooded little Spanish *senoritas* out there in California." She snuggled against him, then moved and let one of her breasts hang invitingly over his mouth.

He was smiling, all thoughts of sleep gone for the night.

"Anything you say, Valerie. For as long as my strength holds out. You've turned into quite a vamp yourself, do you realize that? Valerie the Vamp. I should have known all along."

She stopped him from talking the best way she knew how. She lowered a breast slowly into his mouth, and Spur's eyes sparkled as he settled down, contentedly chewing.